In the Face of All Things Unknown

SHILPE NANDA

Copyright © 2021 by Shilpe Nanda. All rights reserved.

This book or any portion thereof may not be reproduced or used in any manner whatsoever without the express written permission of the publisher except for the use of brief quotations in a book review.

Any reference to historical events, real people, or real places are used fictitiously. Names, characters, and places are products of the author's imagination.

Cover image by: RKM Designs
Illustrations by: Stella Hong
Book design by: SWATT Books Ltd

Printed in the United Kingdom
First Printing, 2021

ISBN: 978-1-9196346-0-9 (Paperback)
ISBN: 978-1-9196346-1-6 (eBook)
ISBN: 978-1-9196346-2-3 (Hardback)

Third Eye Panda
info@thirdeyepanda.com
www.thirdeyepanda.com

For my son Dhyaan,
the light of my life.

ACKNOWLEDGEMENTS

To Mum, Dad, Reena and Amit. Thank you for your unwavering love, support, and guidance in all that I do.

To my son Dhyaan. Thank you for your love, patience and always inspiring me to be a better human being.

Thank you to my friends Alison and Kashyap, who gave me the encouragement to pick up the pen and write, and the gentle support and required critique, when needed.

Thank you to Sam at SWATT Books and Mark at Lexicon, for your wonderful guidance and making this all happen.

In the Face of All Things Unknown

CHAPTER 1

Falling asleep under the warmth of my duvet, I could hear Dad's calming voice as he finished reading my bedtime story. This was my favourite time of the day, when Dad would come home from work, tuck me into bed and read to me. "Okay sweetheart, we have an early start tomorrow as we need to catch our flight early in the morning. You must get some sleep now". "But Daddy, why are we going to India? I am going to miss my friends at school." "We've been through all this Beta (child). It's an important trip, to be at your uncle Arun's wedding. You will now finally meet your mother's side of the

family. Don't worry. You will have plenty of company there. In fact, you will have a great time."

The next day came around quickly. The early morning sky was still so dark, but the roads were flooded by the light from the streetlamps. As we made our way to Heathrow Airport, we drove through Westminster and past the Houses of Parliament. I listened out for the chimes of Big Ben, as the hands of the clock struck 5am. I wasn't used to being up so early. In fact, the lack of sleep was making me feel nauseous as my stomach churned and to add to it, I was also feeling nervous and excited too. I had never been on a plane before. Well, not since I was a baby, and this place called 'India' was quite an unknown mystery to me. I could see the Union Jack standing high in all its full glory. How beautiful the city seemed. So tranquil at that early hour, and so elegant.

My mind began to ponder over what India would be like, and my cousins whom I had never met before. Born into an Indian, Punjabi family, we lived together with our extended family within our large Victorian home. Our home was made up of my uncle (Dad's younger brother), his wife and two children, together with my grandfather, whom we called 'Dadaji' (paternal grandfather). Dad's side of the family hailed from Kenya, East Africa. East African Indians in the UK were known for their abilities in enterprise and initiative, especially when it came to business. During Margaret Thatcher's 1980s enterprise economy, this buoyant community of businessmen thrived and excelled and secured a strong foothold, especially within the retail sector around London. My father was amongst these men. A sterling man who epitomised the virtues of dedication, hard work, consistency, and family values. Having hailed from a family who were twice immigrants themselves, first to Kenya and then England, he recognised the importance of reinventing oneself and continually moving with the times. Mum was a devoted wife to my dad and mother to me and Mina, my younger baby sister, who was only six months old at that time. She hailed from Amritsar, a small city in the state of Punjab. My mother's culinary skills had secured her reputation for being quite a chef. People who visited our home would relish any delicacies made lovingly by her hands. I was their first born and therefore the eldest grandchild in our family home, with Mina being the youngest and the apple of everyone's eye. She was an adorable baby, not particularly fussy and always sporting a smile.

The plane journey seemed to go on forever, and then we finally arrived in New Delhi. As soon as I stepped out of the airport, the overwhelming smell and heat hit me. A rude awakening from the sleepy state that I was in. I was thousands of miles away from home, in a country that many would call their own, and yet it felt alien to me. As we scuttled into the taxi, we passed through the congested streets of New Delhi. I soaked up the overwhelming views from my window. The humidity was penetrating and made me feel uncomfortable even though we were travelling in an air-conditioned car. Despite the chaotic traffic, the taxi arrived at the train station in time for our train journey to Amritsar, home of my maternal grandparents. Uncle Arun also lived with them in their home and had no plans to move out. This was in line with Indian tradition back then, where a son very rarely left his parents' home. Often, when married, his wife would also join him and they would even go on to have children, with three generations, sometimes even four, all living under the same roof. This particularly benefited the eldest and the youngest generations of the family through somewhat of a symbiotic dynamic. The grandchildren benefited from the patience, wisdom, love and attention of the grandparents, and in turn, the grandparents benefited from the energy, laughter and sense of purpose and novelty that their grandchildren brought to their lives.

Amritsar felt like a sleepy city, with less commotion compared to Delhi. It had a slower pace of life and had kept its old-world charm intact. As we approached their home, I felt nervous. I hadn't met them before, as meeting them as a baby didn't quite count for much, well, not to me anyway. As we walked through their front door, it was a little awkward at first. The family had gathered in the living room. They had been eagerly anticipating our arrival all day. I felt my face being scanned and my mannerisms being observed. Perhaps, just like me, they were also looking to see how we were similar and how we were not.

As the days passed, I seemed to ease into my new surroundings. Despite the fact that my Hindi was far from perfect, I was determined to not let the language barrier prevent me from getting to know my family members. Although they all understood English, the domestic staff couldn't, and they found it so amusing when I would speak in English to them, because they couldn't understand. Needless to say, it forced me to learn Hindi much quicker than I had ever imagined to be possible. Before we knew it, the celebrations for my uncle's wedding were in full swing at my grandparent's home. The veranda had been adorned with saffron-coloured garlands made of vibrant marigolds. Dozens of people swarmed through the gates of their home and onto the driveway, where they enjoyed the fresh food being prepared by the chefs who had been especially engaged to cater for the event. There was a large metallic drum filled to the brim with Indian sweets called 'besan ladoos'. They were quite different from my usual chocolate treats that I was accustomed to eating at home, but they were delicious nonetheless. They were the size of golf balls and could easily fit into the palm of my small hands. I can still recall the sweet taste and the sandy, gritty texture of the ladoos on my tongue.

Once all the wedding guests had gathered at the house, they all took to the street to form a procession called a baraat and leave for the wedding venue. As tradition would have it, the groom (who would be mounted on a horse), would lead the procession, whilst the other guests would follow him on foot, to the place where the wedding nuptials had been arranged to take place. In my uncle's case, the elders of the family had arranged for a large marquee to be put up in the lawn of their local gymkhana club. This was where the Hindu wedding ceremony was to be held. 'Gymkhana' was very much an old British colonial term used for clubs where people would gather to socialise, eat, drink, play sport and celebrate.

In the Face of All Things Unknown

As the procession arrived at the club, the wedding band welcomed my uncle's baraat by playing traditional wedding songs to befit the joyous occasion. The loud music could be heard throughout the neighbourhood and there was an undeniable buzz in the air. My mother excitedly met all her long-lost relatives and friends that she hadn't seen in years. "Here are my two daughters", she would tell them. "Isha is six, but going on ten", she laughed, "and my little Minoo (Mina) is just six months old". As the celebrations carried on into the early hours of the morning, my younger cousins and I took full advantage of our parents' distraction and played until our hearts were content and our legs could hold our weight no more.

Strangely to me, there was something very liberating about India. There were fewer rules to follow and people there seem to live from the heart, a lot more than what I was accustomed to. I liked it. The quintessential Indian traits were the free-flowing exchanges of love and warmth between people which were plain for all to see. There was no end to the warmth of the great Indian hospitality being showered down. Whether it was through food or through exchanges of affection, it was undeniable. This was also my grandmother's way of showering me with her love. She would prepare for me my favourite foods and would always make sure I was comfortable and well looked after. I felt safe and warm when I was with her. I felt a sense of belonging and a feeling of being 'rooted', in a way that I had never felt.

The following morning, I was exhausted due to aching limbs from all the excitement and running around from the day before. Nani, my maternal grandmother, called me over and sat me down beside her. "Come, Beta, bring that coconut oil from my dressing table and let me give you a head massage – you will feel much better and get so much relief." As Nani massaged the oil into my hair, she would tell me how this ancient Indian tradition was the secret to how Indian women maintained their tresses, to have flowing beautiful hair. Nani had the most comforting presence about her. Always dressed in a sari and with her hair swept neatly into a bun, she was very much the gentle, Indian matriarch who efficiently orchestrated the running of the

In the Face of All Things Unknown

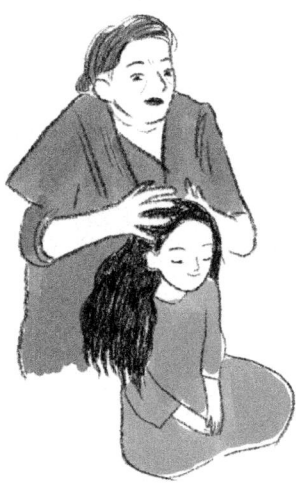

household with complete precision and efficiency. She was the centre of her family's little universe, ensuring that each member of her brood was seen to and was keeping well. Nani would start the day with her daily ritual of offering prayers to her favourite Hindu goddess, Durga. However, before she would sit down at her bedroom shrine in the morning, she would take a bath and only present her 'clean self' before the goddess. She would then light an incense stick, the scent of which would fill the entire house with the calming floral tones of frangipani and sandalwood. This scent would especially linger onto Nani's sari and hair for the entire day and so in my mind's eye her very essence became meshed with that of the goddess Durga, who resided in Nani's bedroom shrine. I remember that night, sleeping in Nani's bed. We would often speak until the early hours of the morning. I had so much to say to her and so much to ask her but somehow the questions wouldn't flow from my mouth as quickly as my mind would form them. Every sentence had to be carefully constructed and considered beforehand. Although when she spoke to me in Hindi my mind understood it all, I couldn't, however, reciprocate with fluency when responding to her. It was frustrating. She didn't speak English either, but I understood her language of love, and then, somehow, the silence didn't seem to matter so much. Nani would often tell me tales of my mother and her siblings when they were younger. She would whisk me off to a nostalgic land of stories that would comfort me before I would sleep. My mother's childhood experiences, growing up in Amritsar, were clearly very different to mine, but that's what made the stories all the more enchanting to hear. Mum always seemed so distracted and preoccupied, rushing around in her daily chores, but Nani was always there. She was that constant steady force, present with me both in mind and body. She would listen to every word I would say intently, just as I would listen to her. Little did I know that in years to come, it would be these bedtime chats that would remain with me and that I would turn to for comfort.

In the Face of All Things Unknown

A week after the wedding, my uncle returned from his honeymoon with his new bride. I was so excited to see my new aunty. Aunty Tanvi was a young bride. She was beautifully dressed in a new silk sari and adorned in gold jewellery. She called me over to her and said, "Open your hand, Isha, and look what I have brought you back from Rishikesh". She placed the most beautiful carving of a figure, made of sandalwood, into the palms of my hand. The fragrance of the sandalwood was hypnotic. I escaped the grown-ups and went and sat on the steps in the hallway. As I wondered at this magnificent little thing in my hands, I thought what a beautiful face he had. I found myself in awe of this man-God called Krishna whose gentle lips were delicately playing the flute. He had wide eyes shaped like lotus petals and wore a peacock feather in his hair. Krishna was the God of compassion, tenderness and love, and perhaps the most widely revered among the Hindu divinities. It seemed that I too had fallen for Krishna's charm, because from that very moment when I had laid eyes on him, Krishna came with me everywhere and became my steady companion and my friend. As the wedding celebrations wrapped up in Amritsar, we bade farewell and continued onto the last leg of our journey.

The atmosphere in Bombay was a rich fusion of colour, heritage and commerce, which made it seem more electric than Amritsar. There was an exciting energy in the air that made you feel so alive. The constant commotion never allowed you to feel lonely in this city, not even for a minute. There were people everywhere, in a rush to get somewhere and do something. It seemed as though the city never slept. In the eighties, visiting India as a foreigner meant standing out like a sore thumb by looking so different from the locals, simply by the clothes that you wore. It was a time when international clothing brands hadn't reached India's shores, and so the locals could tell you as a tourist or visitor from a mile away by what you were wearing. The fascination for foreigners didn't just stop at staring – in fact, the children from the slums would come and touch me and tug at my arm to get my attention. They didn't mean me any harm. They simply wanted to have the chocolate I would be eating or the toy I would be holding in my hand. Of course, I wasn't used to groups of children and adults gathering around me and my family. Nor was I used to being followed like this. For them it was a mixture of fascination and hoping they would get lucky in case we obliged their requests. Sometimes it was fun being the centre of so much attention, but at other times it would also feel overwhelming when they would follow you down a street and watch you so intently. I would often cling to my mother tightly, as I feared losing her in the noisy crowd. However, she was completely unphased by it all. Having grown up in India, she had seen it all before.

In the Face of All Things Unknown

We headed to the ISKCON (International Society for Krishna Consciousness) temple in Juhu. Upon hearing our English accent, a European-looking man clad in saffron robes walked over to us. "Hi there, I recognised the accent and thought I'd come and say 'hello.'" We were naturally somewhat surprised to come across this blonde-haired Englishman who was dressed in the attire of a Hindu ascetic and was sporting the mark of the tilak on his forehead. The 'tilak', which is shaped like the prong of a tuning fork, is made by using a cream-coloured clay called gopi-candana. I was of course intrigued by these markings, that so many other men and women also had adorned on their foreheads. I wanted to know what they meant and so I asked him. He told me that they were a symbol of their love and surrender to Krishna. My parents were intrigued by this well-spoken gentleman hailing from the Cotswolds, who had given up a life of comparable luxury to live a life of self-imposed poverty and self-discipline, to follow his calling as an ascetic. "The life of a Hare Krishna can't be easy, so what has brought you here to India, my friend?" asked my father. "It was simple. The main attraction that brought me here was a sense of belonging. I had travelled the world for well over six years, chasing after and longing for something. I wasn't sure what it was at first, but the void that it left within me left a crushing pain. I tried to ease the pain with many things. I partied hard, had numerous partners, and even turned to substance and alcohol abuse, but nothing seemed to fill that void. That was until I landed at the doorstep of this temple, which at first I thought was a chance encounter, but perhaps landing up here had been divinely orchestrated by a power which at that time was beyond my understanding. What I had been searching for all along was there in front of me, like a gift waiting to be unravelled. Perhaps it is something that is understood less but felt more. To surrender to Krishna, one must be led by the heart and not the mind, and then you too will feel this bliss if you desire to. Come, let me show you around and tell you a little more about this place."

As we walked around, the Englishman enlightened us further. "This temple is dedicated to the divine union between the Hindu deities Radha-Krishna. These two names are spoken together, as though they are one. Such is their love story that they are considered incomplete without the other and believed to be two halves of one soul. Radha being the divine feminine and Krishna the divine masculine of the two. They never married and yet their love was incapable of being destroyed by anything or anyone. What they shared was the embodiment of the highest level of love, in its purest form. This is what they call 'Divine love'. To understand their love is to feel the divine bliss of connecting with God and all his creation. This starts at source, by having Divine love for oneself which then transcends into

In the Face of All Things Unknown

universal love for everything and everyone. For the everyday man this signifies the deep longing of one's soul to connect with the Divine Creator. However, one must remain unattached and love without conditions. Give them the liberty to be free and to be just as they are."

My little mind was confused, to say the least. At such a tender age I could not comprehend a lot of what he was saying, but it had intrigued me, nonetheless. The Englishman looked bemused at my slightly confused expression and said, "Although Krishna was married to Rukmini, the love that Radha had for her beloved remained undeterred despite there being a physical distance between them. She was entirely devoted in her love for Krishna and yet she remained unattached to him. Perhaps it was the distance between them and

Radha's longing for Krishna which made her love him with more intensity. Such was the divine nature of her love that it had no 'want' and expected nothing in return, just as God loves us, unconditionally. Perhaps loving God is just the same. Just as Radha merges with Krishna in this way, it is the constant thought and longing for our creator that helps us merge with him and realise the divine within ourselves. He resides within our heart and soul just as Krishna resides within Radha. We cannot be separated, we are one."

CHAPTER 2

I can clearly recall my long walks to school every morning. Each season came with its own beauty and autumn was undoubtedly my favourite. Walking the streets of London every morning on the way to school, I can remember the crunching of the crisp leaves and horse chestnuts beneath my feet. The leaves on the trees looked beautiful, as though the golden colours of nature had come alive, just before bidding farewell to yet another year. There was always excitement in the air around this time of the year. My birthday would soon be approaching, as was Diwali, followed by the festivities for Christmas. Endless hours were spent creating and then editing my wish list for Christmas presents. Self-indulgence at that age never seemed to come with the same guilt that it does now. That particular year, some days after Diwali had passed, we were returning home after visiting some relatives. It was around 1am, and Mina and I were fast asleep in the back of the car. As we were approaching our home, I woke to the sound of my parents' frightened voices. I wanted to see what the fuss was about and, as I looked out of my window, I understood the reason behind the fear in their voices. Three men were standing outside our front door and were trying to break into our home. They had a large hammer in their hands and the intimidating expressions on their faces really frightened me. Panicked by what he had just witnessed, Dad decided to drive off, away from the scene and out of harm's way. Dad found a phone box and alerted the police. For the next ninety minutes or so, we circled the streets of London as we waited for the police to turn up and tend to the scene. I remember so clearly sitting in the back seat of the car the whole time whilst shivering with fear. Mina and I were so young and impressionable when this incident happened that it somehow eroded the sense of security that I used to feel whilst being at home. We now all felt a sense of vulnerability, especially during the night.

Just as the dust seemed to settle after this incident, our sense of vulnerability and safety was again tested.

Mum came to collect me from school one day, a few hours earlier than usual. I had a doctor's appointment booked for a much-needed vaccination and was excited to be leaving school early that day – however, that excitement was short-lived. As Mum walked through the school playground towards my classroom, she could sense that she was being followed by someone. She turned around and saw a dishevelled-looking man who was trying to catch up with her. Feeling uneasy, she decided to quicken her steps, but before she could reach my classroom door, he grabbed hold of her and tried to pull off the gold necklace that she was wearing around her neck. My mother started to scream for help, and he struggled to break the necklace from her neck, and so he pulled harder. Finally, a small child opened the classroom door and stepped outside into the playground. The man saw this and became alarmed that someone had been alerted to his whereabouts and so he ran off towards the street without managing to take my mother's gold necklace. My mother was naturally very shaken up by this ordeal and was in pain, as the necklace had cut into her skin whilst he was struggling to pull it from her neck. I remember sitting in the headmistress's office as the police took my mother's account and wrote down their report of the incident.

It may have been that this was the last straw, because soon after this incident my family decided it was time to leave behind the rough streets of south London and start life once again someplace else. We moved an hour outside of London to a small town called Walter's Green. I was aged around ten at the time.

It was a really "white" suburban area and was so unlike the cosmopolitan London that I so loved and craved. This place felt alien to me, and I think I was alien to this place too. The area was dull. It wasn't vibrant like London. The energy and vibe here were of a slow-paced, middle-aged town that didn't like change, and our brown faces were an unfamiliar (and maybe even unwelcome) change to the locals' expectations of normality. My parents had bought a run-down shop from an old lady who was looking to retire. The decor was something out of the 1960s and there was a dated, small, two-bedroom flat above the shop, where we were to live for the next seven years. It was so unlike the charming, eight-bedroom period home that we had left behind in London. I was living outside of London for the first time, and in a new area which I didn't like and was not used to. To add to my troubles, I had joined a new primary school where I had a lot of difficulty settling in and making new friends. With no one to talk to at school, and my parents far too busy with their own financial worries, I started to feel quite isolated and alone. I began to really miss my old school friends and teachers and would often write to them during the first few months of having moved. How much I craved to be back with them all.

In the Face of All Things Unknown

My new school was unfortunately totally different. This ten-year-old was the brown-skinned pariah in a room full of white kids. It was unfamiliar territory for me because my old school was so ethnically diverse and colourful. I missed the variety and the excitement of London. My parents' new business seemed to be struggling too. Despite working seven days a week they still struggled to make ends meet. Up until this point, I had never given money a second thought, as all my needs and wants had been provided for responsibly by my parents. But now I could sense the lack. They had begun to speak of the mounting bills and their shortage of money. We had always seemed to have everything we needed but now things appeared quite different. The financial pressure took its toll on my parents, and yet somehow they managed to run this shop seven days a week and find the energy to raise their children, all with little complaint. However, I could see that they were always very tired and sometimes they too seemed a little fed up and stuck by their circumstances, but they never gave up.

Fortunately, as time went on, the local white neighbourhood became quite fond of our family, and Mina and I would very often be invited by our neighbours, Mr and Mrs Fernsby, to play in their garden. We never really had a garden to play in. It was more a yard which had nothing much growing in it other than rhubarb and weeds, so being invited to play in the Fernsbys' garden was a rare treat for us that we relished and really looked forward to. Across the street from us lived another friendly couple, Mr and Mrs Grewal. Theirs was an inter-racial marriage, as Mr. Grewal was a Sikh who hailed from New Delhi. His work had brought him to England in the 1950s which is where he met Muriel, an English woman. Much to the dismay of their family, they decided to marry and settle down together in England. Although Muriel's mother was blind, she was very much disturbed by the fact that her daughter had married a man of colour. Every year, Mr and Mrs Grewal would invite us to their home for Christmas lunch. This was the perfect opportunity for them to enlighten us with endless tales of their love story.

As time went on, we had slowly become accepted and welcomed by the locals. I had even begun to enjoy my primary school and make new friends. Once again, I had found my sense of belonging within my new environment, and with time my confidence and happiness slowly returned.

Hailing from an affluent Arab background, Dahlia was one of my new friends. She was crazy beyond belief and so much fun to be around. Dahlia would take me away from my own troubles. She was artistic, eccentric, and uninhibited in being her authentic self. I admired this about her and found her, in many ways, to be courageous. When together, we would laugh for hours on end. I often wished that I could be free-spirited

like Dahlia. We would ride our mountain bikes everywhere around the neighbourhood, just to escape our parents. This would often be to the cinema, the local burger joint or to Blockbuster video to hire the latest Hollywood films and watch them back-to-back. I never was quite sure what antics she would get up to on any day, as they were sometimes hilarious and sometimes quite embarrassing, but she was always up for having harmless fun.

Two streets away from Dahlia's home lived Graham Watts. Dahlia and I would often cycle down to his house to see what he was up to. Graham had strawberry blonde hair and freckles around his nose. He came dressed impeccably for school every single day. With his crisp white collared shirts and without a hair out of place, he looked like a poster boy for Marks and Spencer with his wholesome boyish looks. We were in the same class and he sat across the table from me, which made it quite convenient to play footsie under the table whilst our teacher Mr. Roberts would look on in our direction and yet be completely oblivious to our antics. Sometimes he would pull my ponytail as he would walk behind my chair, or he would nudge me when we would cross each other in the classroom. I enjoyed being teased by Graham and relished the attention that I got from him.

That year, it seemed as though the summer came and went so quickly. As I lapped up the last few days with Graham and Dahlia, I knew that things were about to change between us, and it wouldn't be the same anymore. With the autumn months looming ahead, the three of us would now be going off to separate high schools, which marked the beginning of a new era in our lives and in our seemingly innocent childhood. Dahlia's parents could afford to send her to an exclusive girls' school called Reddington Hill. It was a Catholic school run by the Irish nuns who lived at the convent there. Graham was going on to St. Marks, a Church of England school. I, on the other hand, went on to 'Elmhurst Comprehensive'. With more than a thousand children, the size of the school was quite daunting to me at first. Many of the kids came from dysfunctional families and at school they were often quite disruptive and rude towards the teachers. Bullying was commonplace too. Sadly, school was their outlet to release their unhappiness. Being a sensitive soul, I very often felt out of my depth at this school because the atmosphere felt hostile. You knew it was only a matter of time until you would be the next person to be picked on by one of the bullies. There weren't many brown faces either at this school. We were a stark minority and were very much aware of this at all times. It was commonplace for even my so-called friends to throw racist jibes at me in jest, in an effort to appear 'cool' in front of the rest of the class. Subconsciously us 'brown kids' were always on tenterhooks, waiting to be called a "Paki" or being told to return back home to where we came from. This was the standard racist blow one might have been subjected to whilst growing up in 1990s Britain. Often, the comments would be unprovoked and unexpected, sometimes whilst walking down a school corridor or walking down a street. However, they were piercing enough to ruin not just your day, but your entire week. The irony was that England was where I was born and the only country that I had ever called 'home'. It was all that I knew. However, coming from a family that wished to preserve its Indian and somewhat conservative values, I often felt caught up in an identity crisis, with no real sense of belonging.

Shilpe Nanda

In an effort to protect me from the outside, corrupt world of drugs, substance abuse and teenage pregnancies, my parents reacted by limiting my personal freedom to the extent that I sometimes felt suffocated. I wanted to spread my wings and fly but all I could do was go running, and that too came with restrictions. Running for the athletics team at school was where I found my release for my pent-up frustration and I tried to do this as often as I could. But just like my friends, what I really wanted was to be hanging out until late with friends at shopping malls and parties. Instead, spending time with friends was, in reality, limited to me hanging out with three or four of my closest friends who lived in the neighbourhood, and whom I could visit in their home, or ride my mountain bike with. Very quickly, as a teenager, I found myself in the most bizarre paradoxical situation whereby although England had always been my home, I was no longer sure just how at home I felt in England anymore.

I started to question my identity and my sense of belonging, because at school I was reminded I was 'different' and the subliminal vibe that I got from my parents was also not that dissimilar. I was constantly reminded that a good Indian girl should behave in a respectable way. The tyranny of not being allowed out much started to get to me. My friends grew tired of asking me to hang out with them at weekends, because they quickly learnt that their invitations would only be met with rejection. At first I was upset, but this quickly turned to relief because I no longer had to face the embarrassment of making up another excuse as to why I was the only one in our group who couldn't join the group social. However, with time, my feelings of loneliness often felt crippling, as I longed to experience the same things as my friends and those of any other thirteen-year-old teenager. With the financial pressures of the business mounting, Mum and Dad were too busy arguing between themselves to notice what was going on with me. They seemed completely oblivious to my internal struggles, as they had so many other pressures and I didn't know how to discuss these feelings with them either and so I held it all in.

Already feeling quite alone and isolated, I guess this is how the feelings of disconnection with people and the outside world began. With no one to talk to and nowhere to go, rage began to fill my head and my heart. Its release came in the form of constant self-critical chatter inside my mind. It just wouldn't stop. When I looked in the mirror, I hated the person staring back at me. She didn't feel worthy or lovable to anyone, especially not to me. I thought I was fat and ugly, and therefore I was unlovable. Perhaps it was a lack of self-acceptance and self-love that led me to develop an unhealthy relationship with myself. There was no in-between, nor was there any balance. I simply didn't understand what I was doing to myself emotionally. I felt so confined and suffocated, that I wanted to escape my reality into the vastness of the world. I longed to experience life and not just imagine it inside my head, in my make-believe world, where I would attend parties and have boyfriends like all the other kids my age were doing. My imagination would transport me anywhere with anyone. Perhaps it was safer this way, for I wouldn't run the risk of getting hurt.

CHAPTER 3

It was a Sunday morning and the family had just finished eating breakfast when we received the phone call from my uncle informing us that my paternal grandfather (Dadaji) had just died in his sleep. He had had a larger-than-life persona which dominated any room that he was in. His presence commanded the attention, not only of family but also of his peers. Such was his nature and reputation, that at his funeral, people spoke of him with regard and remembered him as a key member within our community. Although at times I felt a little intimidated by him and was scared to get on his bad side as he was quick to anger, we still shared a special bond.

It was our love of books and history that connected us. He encouraged and praised us even for the smallest of academic achievements. In many ways this helped to propel me into higher education. I knew how proud he would have been had he lived to see me qualify as a lawyer. Even today, I am still very much the eternal scholar on a relentless quest for answers, from myself, from the universe and about my existence itself. The questions never end, and the answers are many. Being as young as I was, I was naturally terribly upset by his death and I became fearful, especially at night. Mum and Dad dealt with their grief in their own way. Dad threw himself into his work and Mum did the same too.

Mum was always wonderful at making sure we were always beautifully dressed, well fed, and that we behaved impeccably, especially in front of others. Her love was exhibited through her unwavering and dutiful service to her family. That was what being a good mother and wife meant to her. She struggled talking about emotions because she had locked hers away. It was the only way she knew how to survive and cope with the loneliness and heartache of living thousands of miles away from her family back home in India. Her marriage to my father was an arranged one. Fortunately, theirs was a happy and successful marriage built on the premise of enduring love and support for one another and their children.

Meanwhile, my discontent at Elmhurst Comprehensive had grown, as I had become increasingly unhappy there. As time had gone on, the racist comments began to really pierce my heart and knock my confidence. Before I had even realised, relationships had become a source of insecurity for me. I had started to form a picture quite early on in my head that people couldn't be relied upon. If you got too close, they could be a potential source of pain which I needed to shield myself from. I had convinced myself it was only a matter of time before I would end up getting hurt, and so my heart began to close a little. I decided it wasn't safe to let people in.

Unlike before, my parents had now become acutely aware of this and could see just how unhappy I was, so when they came across an advertisement in the local newspaper for places in the same exclusive school as my friend Dahlia, they decided to put me forward for one of them. I took the entrance exam and fortunately, I managed to secure a scholarship at the school. 10th December 1992. I remember the day vividly, as this was the day when the letter came through our letterbox informing us of this good news.

The school building was perched handsomely on top of the hill, where it stood in all its magnificent glory. Built in the 18th century, the historic building was surrounded by six hundred acres of manicured lawns and playing fields. The view from the hill was breathtaking, and on a clear day we had a generous view of the town of Reddington. However, the building which always caught my eye was St. Benedict's Abbey. The church was designed in an eclectic and flamboyant gothic style and hence it stood out despite the trees that seemed to get in the way. The abbey was a contemplative monastery of the Benedictine order. The monks would work on a busy farm and operate a printing and publishing house. The Benedictine Community of Monks was a closed order, and the vast majority of monks were not permitted to speak or converse with guests due to their vow of silence. This made their world seem more secretive, aloof and cut-off from ours and in many ways it was. Their world was far removed from the one that we lived in. However, there were some monks (who were solemnly professed), that were assigned to be responsible for ensuring that 'all guests who present themselves' at the abbey were to be received and 'welcomed as Christ'. Occasionally, these solemnised monks were permitted to venture away from the abbey and visit the staff at our school, which was predominantly made up of Irish nuns. On these infrequent days, we would see the monks walking up the hill in their long dark habits towards the school and going for long walks with the nuns on the school grounds. Of course, as students we found this to be hugely entertaining and were eager to catch a nun and monk amid a rendezvous. However, to the best of my knowledge, this never happened whilst I was a pupil at Reddington Hill, or at least, no one was ever caught! This did not halt the search for corroborating evidence and produced endless speculation and entertainment for many students.

The school grounds and building had an old-England charm about them, which oozed class and sophistication. It was a highly exclusive school where the kids were groomed to be different and to become high achievers. It felt all a little surreal and at first and I certainly felt as though I was a fish out of water, but it was all very exciting nonetheless. Meanwhile, I joined the athletics team at school. Running made me feel happy. I felt free and liberated and the rush of adrenaline gave me a natural high. I soon found myself training and running every evening after school.

I began to really like my new school and my new friends, and before I knew it, I started to feel settled. Although it was a Catholic girls' school, the lack of boys helped us to enjoy our youth a little longer. We grew into our adolescence with the comfort of knowing that there were no boys on site that we had to look 'cool' in front of, or 'pretty' for. Nor did we feel pressured into losing our virginity too prematurely or having a boyfriend just for the sake of it. In fact, we were free, and we were uninhibited and the only romantic notions running through our minds were fantasies of our favourite rock bands, Guns N' Roses and Bon Jovi. MTV was of course our quickest portal to transport us to our world of rock n' roll fantasies. Not only were we on the whole quite studious and ambitious girls, but there was also a streak of creative genius within many of us and the school helped to cultivate this even further.

Some excelled in music, drama and theatre, whilst others excelled in debating and public speaking. It was on the whole a very 'British School' and, in keeping with its traditions that spanned over three centuries, its students were cultivated to become 'cultured, well-mannered ladies with etiquettes that were hallmarked by an understated confidence and elegance'. My immediate circle of friends within my class were a group of five girls. One of them was Anna, a beautiful blonde-haired pop-star princess in the making. She was vocally talented and equally just as pretty. Us girls would often laugh, joke, and sing out loud together, as though no one was watching. We amused ourselves endlessly with silly 'dares' and were quite fascinated by the idea of trying to solve the mystery of locating the 'nuns' graveyard'. It was believed that when a nun would first join the convent at Reddington Hill, she would take solemn vows that she would spend an entire lifetime there and live a life of prayer and contemplation and being actively devoted to educating the girls at our school. Rumour had it that in keeping with their vows, this meant that they were also buried in the school grounds, in a secret graveyard, somewhere amongst the six hundred acres that belonged to the school. We often escaped into the unpermitted areas of the school grounds in an effort to resolve this mystery. However, unfortunately our efforts bore no fruit as we never did quite establish where the graveyard was located.

Life seemed to finally be on the up, until about a year into attending my new school, I came to learn that behind my back, Anna had made a very mean-spirited and racist comment about me to our mutual circle of friends. It took me by complete and utter surprise that she had referred to me as a "black person in a white country." In fact, I had never even thought that she could make such a comment. However, I was devastated and couldn't believe that someone whom I considered to be a friend would behave this way. My faith in people had now sunk even lower, but this time it threw me even further back down that slippery slope of loneliness. This world felt like a mean and hostile place and I wasn't sure if I could trust people anymore, especially since time kept proving to me over and over again that once you let people 'in', they only hurt you.

I was now more lost than ever and became suspicious of my 'innocent' friends too. I began to isolate myself as much as I could, as a way to protect my heart. But this made me angry. I was now angry at home around my family, and angry at school. For the first time, this otherwise very obedient and sweet-natured young girl had started to become rebellious in her outlook on life. The rage filled up inside her head and her heart. Little did I know or realise at the time, but I was depressed. I found little joy in life. I would often lay awake at night until the early hours of the morning, with my bedroom window cast wide open just to experience the cold air blowing on my face and feeling alive. The night sky looked so beautiful, and I often felt envious of its tranquillity and peace. Something I had never felt within. I would ask God, "Why me?" Why was I going through so much inner turmoil and pain? I wanted it to stop but I didn't know how. I didn't understand why I had always felt so different from everyone else. All my friends seemed so happy and carefree, and I wanted to be just like them, but I wasn't. My longing for love and connection with others was hurting me in ways that I could not imagine. In fact, the hurt ran so deep that I often wished my painful existence would just end. I was only thirteen years old, but life was already proving to be so difficult, and I wasn't sure how I was going to navigate my way through it. As I began to build thick walls around my heart, something inside of me had now changed. I started to question my place in the world and my identity. I was lost between two cultures. I belonged to both but wasn't fully accepted by either of them. My loneliness and lack of meaningful connection with people gave me dark thoughts of sadness which hung over me like a heavy, grey cloud and followed me everywhere. I began to isolate myself and would prefer to be in the safe company of myself than that of others.

As the school term came to a close and the Easter holidays approached, my mother managed to lure me into taking a five-week trip to India, where I would travel alone and stay with my relatives. I agreed and was so excited by the opportunity. Those five weeks when I was away in India gave me the emotional headspace to get some down-time and clarity. I finally began to tune into myself again. There was something so soothing about being around my family in India, especially Nani and Nana (my maternal grandfather). When I was with them, I felt safe and I felt an innate sense of peace. There was just a wonderful abundance of love, care and tenderness which was what my soul so desperately needed, to heal and to get better, and to drop the anger that had consumed me. I had often heard that the universe sends us exactly what we are ready for and at the exact time that we need it in our lives and so, as fate would have it, I found myself visiting one of the most revered places of Hindu pilgrimage in India. It is a sacred temple called Vaishno Devi, which nestles among the Trikuta Hills, in the most northerly Indian state of Jammu and Kashmir. This trip was not planned at all. In fact, I had been invited by a distant aunt who I had never met before in my life, and yet I felt compelled to go on this adventure with her.

They say that one cannot visit the holy temple until one receives the spiritual call (bulaawa) of Vaishno Devi herself. The Goddess had invited me to her holy abode so that I could begin my journey of healing from within. The trek to the cave temple at the top of the mountain took over eight hours to complete. It felt like an impossible task and yet I was determined to walk all the way up to the top on foot. Somehow, my dogged determination and sheer tenacity got me through, and we managed to reach the cave temple on the first day itself. It is within the cave temple that the Goddess Vaishno Devi is believed to reside. She is the manifestation of Shakti, who is otherwise more commonly known as the Goddess Durga. In Indian cosmology, God is described as having two divine aspects, which are the divine feminine and the divine masculine, otherwise known as Shiva and Shakti. Once we have awakened, we learn to embrace the divine within us and live in balance with our own divine masculine and feminine natures. This is what is called 'God consciousness'.

Tarsem was our tour guide on the pilgrimage. He could sense my bewilderment and excitement at the hordes of thousands of people who had come to Vaishno Devi to receive the Goddess Durga's blessings. Tarsem looked over at me and said, "Durga is the deity to call upon when you're in deep trouble, facing obstacles or fighting your inner demons. She is the power behind our spiritual awakening which unleashes the transformative inner force that helps us evolve our own awareness. To access her, we must surrender to the Goddess and ask for her help." I remembered doing just that. Praying for her help. I wasn't sure what I was praying for or asking, but I knew that I wanted to feel happy and normal again. It was beautiful. Thousands of people coming together in their absolute faith in something that was much bigger than them. Everybody here was in search of something, and some of them had already found it, and were returning to give thanks to Goddess Durga for the benevolence that she had bestowed upon them. I too had found what I was unknowingly looking for. Somehow this trip miraculously cured me of my depression. I finally felt connected with something much bigger and began to feel at peace with who and what I was and once again I began to enjoy life's simple pleasures. I soon gained comfort in my new-found identity. I realised that I no longer needed to pigeon-hole myself into being just British or just Indian, as I was both. I was a 'new breed' – or hybrid culture if you like. I was 'a British national of Indian descent' and it was okay for both countries to be equally dear to me.

CHAPTER 4

I remember vividly being invited to a family dinner party one evening by aunty Sumita. She was my mother's cousin, twice removed. Struggling to come to terms with the breakdown of her own marriage, she was particularly conscious of how the local Indian community in London would perceive her pending divorce and so-called personal failure, as this is what she believed it to be. Therefore, like many other women of that generation, she decided to stay put and remain within the marriage. However, she would often contemplate a life without her husband. Aunty Sumita found me reading alone in another room, away from the noisy adults, and away from the toddlers who were playing out in the garden. I sensed that aunty Sumita was wanting to say something, as though it was quite literally on the very tip of her tongue. And then, suddenly, she blurted it all out. Perhaps it was just that I was a captive hostage for her to vent her woes to. However, I wasn't quite ready for the bombshell she was about to throw at me, and nor did I have a choice.

My aunt, with little thought or concern for my feelings or the consequences, gleefully announced that my mother and uncle had been adopted by my nani and nana when they were very young. And so the story went, nani came across a young woman and her two small children at her local temple. The woman was often found singing devotional songs there, as this would help her provide for her children. When nani enquired about her husband and her family, the woman informed her that she had been married off as a young bride and her husband had died within four years of their marriage. Since his death, she had been left to live in a world that only abused and humiliated widows. The young mother had been thrown out of her marital home by her in-laws because they feared that she would demand a share of the ancestral property. The woman then went to her parents' house, but even her parents had turned against her, not allowing her to enter the main house and socialise with other family members because they believed that widows brought bad luck. She had nowhere else to go with her children and so she came to the temple, seeking refuge.

Nani could not comprehend the injustice of what she was hearing and seeing. The two beautiful children and their mother, who were grieving the loss of a father and husband, now had to also face the onslaught of communal wrath and not to mention, enduring social stigma too.

The woman appeared weak and frail so nana and nani invited her and her children into their home giving them a roof over their heads and shelter. She died some months later from a chronic illness. Whilst on her deathbed, she told nana and nani that she often feared she would die an undignified death and that other than her very small children, nobody would mourn her demise. However, she felt immense gratitude towards my grandparents, as they had welcomed her and her children into their home, where she lived her last days in dignity and not in humiliation.

After her death, nana and nani decided to adopt her children as their own, much to the dismay of their own family and members of their local village, who couldn't understand why they would choose to raise someone else's children. However, this made very little difference to them. Nana and nani were both very ordinary and yet heroic individuals who found the strength to persevere and stand up for what they believed in. They saw past the labels and believed in their love for these children, whom they now considered to be their own.

Following this revelation, my aunt was probably waiting for my reaction, but I wasn't sure how I was meant to react. I naturally remained quiet and listened to everything she said. I had never been made aware of this by my mother and although I was in awe of my grandparents' beautiful and inspiring tale of bravery (and in my opinion heroism), I felt confused at what I was hearing. Perhaps my mother never knew and wasn't aware of her family history. I didn't know what the answer was, but I vowed I would never bring this up again in case she didn't know. I didn't want to cause my mother any sadness on my account.

During that era of 1950s' India, it took true courage to take on the world and to challenge the social norms and values of that time. My grandparents did just that. It is their love that gave my mother and uncle Arun, a safe harbour where they could once again feel protected and cherished, as it shielded them from the wrath of the world. However, one can still question just how much modern-day society has moved on from its regressive views about widowhood , re-marriage and divorce. Even to this day, in many parts of the world, widows are still subjected to deep-rooted patriarchal traditions and religious legislation, which often leaves them leading a life of marginalisation, disadvantage and poverty.

In the Face of All Things Unknown

CHAPTER 5

It was the summer of 1998 and I was preparing to leave home for the first time to start my studies at Cardiff University, where I had secured a place to study law. However, I didn't want to be in Cardiff – I wanted to be in London, the city that I loved the most. I was now miles away from home and rather than enjoying my new-found freedom, I was instead extremely homesick, and missing my family incredibly. In comparison to me, I found my new flatmates to be quite forward and liberated in a way which felt uncomfortable to me. I found myself living with a group of girls who would quite happily come home for some casual sex with a random stranger they had picked up in a nightclub. Having lived such a sheltered childhood, this wasn't something that I was used to and the thought of sleeping with someone who was a stranger petrified me. I was keen to find myself a boyfriend at university, but not that way. I preferred it when things were done in a more tame and organic manner and, fortunately for me, this is how I found Johan, my university sweetheart.

One day, shortly before my eighteenth birthday, to be precise, I was walking through the campus grounds and came across this well-dressed and handsome-looking guy. He had this boyish and yet innocent look about him which only increased his appeal to me. As he walked past me, our eyes met briefly, and we smiled at one another. I was now intrigued and wanted to know more about him. I enquired about him and very quickly established that he was an actuarial science student and that we both had mutual friends. With my birthday only days away, I thought that this would be the perfect excuse to invite him and his friends to my birthday celebrations and that way I could get to know him a little better. The trick seemed to work and after my birthday we began to spend more and more time with each other every day. His feelings towards me grew quite quickly and very soon we became inseparable as a couple. He loved his mother immensely and was close to his siblings. That was very apparent about him from the very beginning, and I respected that about him. Although he was an American, he belonged to the Baha'i faith, which is a religion that teaches the essential worth of all religions, and the unity of all people. He wasn't particularly religious, but I admired that deep respect that he always showed towards all faiths. I felt very safe with him. Johan gave me the anchor that deep-down I desired. He would often listen to my frustrations with family or friends, but he never judged me, nor would he ever complain. His advice to me would be simple and profound, and yet I always welcomed it, because I knew that above everything, he was my best friend, and his advice was coming from a good place. Johan always told me to love my family and friends freely and without any expectations in return. He told me to trust that whatever love I put out in the universe, it would always come back to me tenfold. It would never be wasted.

The third wheel in my relationship with Johan was Daniel West. He was without a shadow of a doubt our closest friend at university and all three of us were joined at the hip, but we liked it that way. We were a little family. Quirky and fun-loving, Daniel was one of those quintessential English men, who spoke the Queen's English and, with his dark good looks and towering frame, was enough to make any woman go weak at the knees. His sexual orientation was plain for all to see, except I had no inkling that he was gay.

There were of course some subliminal vibes, but we never really paid that much attention to them. When he finally chose to come out to us as gay, we were of course surprised by this and a little taken back, but we still loved him all the same. He was 'our friend' and that was all that mattered. I was nobody to judge Daniel on his choice or his lifestyle. I remember thanking him for telling me and applauding his bravery for being true to himself and his courage for speaking up. I could only imagine how difficult life would have been for him whilst leading up to this point. The fear of not being able to express your authentic self and proclaim your sexuality for fear of rejection by those who were close to you. I just wanted him to be happy now, whoever that was with. Daniel often told me that he wished he were straight because that way, life would have been much easier on him. At that point I realised that sexual orientation was not about fantasy or sexual promiscuity – it ran much deeper than that. 'Being gay' came just as naturally to Daniel as 'being straight' was to me.

In my final year of university, I travelled to India alone to visit Nani. Nana had died just a few months earlier, leaving a gaping hole in her life. She was utterly devastated and would often speak of him and the fond memories that they had shared. I listened. There was little else I could do or say to comfort her apart from hug her and give her affection. I could see that her grief had broken her heart and made her so weak. When returning to London I questioned whether this would be the last time that I would ever see her. Three months later, we received the news that Nani had died. This loss was hard. I wished I had been there with her in her last days. There was so much I wished we had spoken about and now I would never have the chance. I had lost that mother figure in my life. That solid trunk from which the family tree had branched out, was felled. It took me a long time to come to terms with my loss. There were often days when I would fall to my knees in grief or wake from my sleep, in tears because my nani would visit me in my dreams, and it would feel so real. Upon waking I would once again remember that she was no more, and that shard of grief would once again pierce my heart. Throughout this time, Johan cared for me like a mother would. He was sensitive and loving. Perhaps at that time I didn't realise the depth of his love for me but now I realise how deep his care really was. I loved Johan but we both knew and understood that once university was over, our ways would part. He never contested this and neither did I. Deep down we both felt that this was for the best, as he would be returning home to Connecticut.

University came to an end and I returned home. I was lost. The best friend that had anchored and shielded me was no longer there to protect me. I naively thought that the best way to get over my pain of losing Johan would be to throw myself into another relationship. I decided to pursue post-graduate studies at University College London (UCL). This is a prestigious university, and I was excited to be studying a Master's degree in law there and being taught by some of the most renowned lecturers in the field. It was around this time that I was introduced, through mutual friends, to a man called Sahil. We used to chat for hours on MSN Messenger and then it progressed to phone calls where we would speak every night, sharing jokes, anecdotes, and hopes for our future dreams and ambitions. I finally met Sahil in person for the first time a month later. I felt disappointed that the chemistry we shared over the phone didn't translate into the same equation when we both were together in person. I forced myself into the relationship, because we had a great understanding and friendship, but there was no spark between us, and I felt disappointed. He knew this deep down and it made me feel guilty, even shallow, but I couldn't fake that feeling. Nor did I want to hurt him by ending things between us because he really was a wonderful and kind person. I carried on with the relationship for maybe just under a year and then I told him the truth – that I couldn't carry on anymore. I selfishly liked the comfort of Sahil being there because, more than anything else, he had always been a sensitive and loving friend and I knew that by ending things between us, I would also lose a great friend. With Sahil no longer in the picture, I once again found myself feeling very lonely and wanting to be in a relationship again, as I believed this was the only way to fill that void within me. I had a tendency of not giving adequate consideration to whether a man was right for me or not, and jumping right in. This tendency was of course beginning to set a pattern for things to come.

CHAPTER 6

Being the fresh, new graduate in the office, I was only too aware of the attention I was getting from some of the younger men. Sameer was one of them. I could feel his eyes scanning the room and following me. Sameer worked as a business development manager within the same company. He would often go to great lengths to get my attention and to flirt with me. One day, we both happened to be in the staff restaurant at the same time. We got talking and he invited me out to attend the opening of a new bar in London with his friends. I was going as his plus one. I guess I was bored and lonely because of everything that had happened only months earlier with my break-up with Sahil, and so I accepted his invitation and went along. I wasn't attracted to him at all at the beginning, although he was fun to be around.

On the train journey back home, he started to open up and he told me about his ex-girlfriend. Her name was Nafisa. Nafisa had apparently cheated on him and left him for a wealthy Indian businessman who was settled in Dubai. This had broken Sameer's heart. The long journey back gave us both an opportunity to share our woes about our respective broken relationships. He didn't seem judgmental of me and didn't make an issue of the boyfriends that I had had in the past either, unlike many other Asian men, who often didn't hesitate in being vocal with their opinions. I liked this about Sameer – he seemed refreshingly open-minded, and unlike other men I had come across, there was an artistic streak in him, and he enjoyed and appreciated the creative arts with a passion, as did I.

When at work, we started to spend more time together and go out for lunch, sometimes just the two of us and sometimes with colleagues too. We often socialised outside of work and slowly I started to really enjoy being with him. It kept me busy, and I was having fun. Something I hadn't done much of whilst growing up. After years of intense studies, I was enjoying the feeling of finally being liberated and just living life in the moment. As the months rolled on, Sameer and I were hanging out more and more. There were feelings of attraction growing between us. At times, we would act like girlfriend and boyfriend and then, suddenly, things between us would switch back to a more neutral and platonic gear. It would get confusing at times – however, we both knew and understood that we were more than just friends.

One thing which was troubling was that his temper could be erratic at times. I remember him raging at me once because I had not invited him to join me for a lunch that I had been invited to by a friend. But then there was this other side to him – fun, seemingly confident, the life and soul of a party, and it was this side that I enjoyed being around. His declarations of love were especially there for public show. I, of course, imagined them to be grand gestures of heartfelt emotions and a love for me that ran deep. I always believed that all Sameer needed was a lot of love from me, which would give him a sense of belonging and make him feel rooted. I thought I would be able to rescue him from his childhood difficulties and that together we would be happy.

Meanwhile, my parents were becoming increasingly inquisitive and wanted to know more about this new man that their daughter was spending so much time with. They had sensed there was more going on between us than I had let on, and so they invited him for lunch. Sameer was very reluctant at first to come home and then he finally did. Sameer tried to cover up his nerves by talking far too much. He came across as overly confident, almost to the point of arrogance. Sameer thought this would impress my father – however, it did the opposite. My parents weren't convinced that he was the right man for me and had strong reservations about him and our suitability as a couple, but I was undeterred from the momentous decision I had made – I wanted to marry him. They eventually gave in reluctantly and came round to the idea.

As per north Indian tradition, the Roka (engagement) ceremony was held at our home with our close relatives present. We were now betrothed to one another. The wedding had been set for 8th December 2006. During the next six months leading up to the wedding, a different side of Sameer became more and more apparent. His mood would swing, and he would lose his temper frequently and without cause. With only a few days to go before the wedding, I called him to discuss the seating plan for our guests. Once more he snapped and yelled at me on the phone because he couldn't deal with the pressure of it all. I began to cry uncontrollably and hyperventilate. It all felt so wrong, even though he had called me back to apologise and tell me that he loved me, but I felt ill at ease and sick to my stomach. In the days leading up to my wedding I was so tense.

I really wished at this time that I could have spoken with my nani. I really missed her and kept wondering what advice she would have given me, because in my heart I felt like I was making a mistake by marrying Sameer. The wedding was now days away and I felt it was too late to back out. My ego was getting the better of me, as I didn't want to face the humiliation of a cancelled wedding. I was about to be married. The invitation cards had been printed and delivered, and my day of reckoning beckoned. Although numb with fear, confused, and crippled by self-loathing and doubt, I suppressed my fears inside sufficiently to press ahead. I married him.

On the day of my wedding, I decided to wear my nani's necklace that she had gifted my mother on her wedding day. I was really missing her presence and felt comforted by wearing something that had once belonged to her. I needed to be reminded that she was close by and with me on this day. I needed her blessings. At the wedding reception, Sameer was very drunk and obnoxiously loud. I felt hugely uncomfortable throughout the day. His behaviour was very erratic and unpredictable, and I didn't understand what was going on with him. He was snappy and aggressive in his tone, not just with me but with some of the guests too. He spent most of the evening getting drunk with his friends and dancing with them. He just didn't seem concerned about his new bride or even her whereabouts. I spent most of the wedding reception dancing at the opposite end of the dancefloor with my family, friends, and relatives because he was too busy having a great time alone with his friends. The series of disappointments that had played out throughout the lead-up to my wedding day had left me feeling saddened and confused. Little did I realise that the phrase "Start as you intend to go on" would hold all too true as an indication of things to come in my marriage.

We went on our honeymoon to the Bahamas. Sameer was seemingly happy on our honeymoon. He was generally kinder and more considerate towards me than I had ever known him to be. I would look forward to cosying up with Sameer and enjoying romantic evenings together, but instead he preferred to sleep. Whenever I reached out for him in the hope that he would hold me tenderly, he would always make some excuse or another to push me away. I desperately longed for that sense of connection with him, but he was indifferent to my feelings. This carried on throughout our time in the Bahamas and the pain of my childhood loneliness came flooding back. I felt myself beginning to fear that this was how the rest of my life would be.

He continued the same behaviour even when we returned home to London. He always seemed emotionally and physically unavailable and not present with me in the marriage. His social calendar was always full. He would drift from one party to another without any respite in between. Life was so hectic with him. It was as though he was constantly on the run, running from himself. He couldn't be still, because that would mean facing up to something deep within himself and I was never sure what that was. There was a pain rooted within him, a void so vast and so deep that nothing could fill it. Not me, not my sincerity nor my care and certainly not my presence. His restless mind was incessantly in search of faults and problems, seeking flaws in my dedication to him or his family. I could not win. Every single day, I would be walking a tightrope, making sure I would not put a foot wrong or else there would be a price to pay. The slightest little trigger for him would come in the form of a comment wrongly perceived, or an oversight on my part, which would culminate in a storm. His mood would change so quickly, and I would anticipate that any wrong move or comment on my part would trigger the onslaught of verbal abuse. And when the attacks came, they were many and from a place of seething reproach. Meeting my family and friends with him would cause me real anxiety. He knew this, and perhaps even enjoyed it a little, because he could say whatever he wanted and taunt me in front of loved ones and just watch me squirm as I tried not to retaliate and create a scene. As time passed, it became easier to just retreat back into myself. I could feel a sense of rage building inside me. I felt angry at being pushed away. I felt angry at not being loved and not being heard, but most of all, what really hurt was not being respected by him.

Soon after marrying Sameer, nothing felt right. There was no sign of that honeymoon period that everybody talked about – in fact it was nowhere to be seen or felt. Everything felt superficial and insincere. I had rushed into marrying him in the hope of finding true love and connection but my God, what had I done? My pain made no difference to him and he carried on leading his bachelor life as though I wasn't there. I was invisible. Why had he married me if he didn't want me there? A sense of confusion started to develop in my mind and that is when my emotional descent began. I decided to stay with my parents for a while, to get some respite, and to figure out what I needed to do with my life. I stayed there for a month and during that time often contemplated leaving Sameer and ending the marriage. In fact, I tried, and I almost did, until his pleas came with the promises that he would change. And as gullible and foolish as I was, I returned to him. Despite his fervent promises, the pattern continued, and Sameer was hardly ever at home with me in the evenings. He would leave me alone almost every night and he would tell me that he had to go and support his friend who was getting divorced at the time. Sameer would make me feel guilty if I asked for any of his time, because my needs were less important than the people that he chose to always prioritise over me. When he was at home with me, he would be making plans to head out somewhere with his friends. I felt hurt and I felt rejected, but most importantly, I didn't feel as though I was enough for him. As time passed, he began to show more and more contempt towards me in front of others, especially when he was drunk. He would flare up at the smallest of things and continued to be chaotic in the way that he would handle his life, his finances, our marriage and even our home. He would bury his head deep in the sand. This would take the form of excessive sleeping and excessive socialising. When I would gently encourage him to see to his mounting credit card debt or ask for his help around the house, his temper would blow up, in a fit of rage. I was still only twenty-seven at the time, but it felt like my shoulders were bearing a very heavy weight. I had very little time or opportunity to have fun as other twenty-seven-year-olds were doing, as I had been thrust into the role of being the person that would 'mop up' the financial mess that he would frequently make, which took the form of excessive debt and expenditure well beyond his means.

Eventually I became so emotionally disturbed that I was unable to switch off from my pain, even whilst I slept. I would often fall asleep wishing that I could turn back the clock to the time before my marriage, when I was carefree and single, as nothing up to this point in my life had prepared me for this marriage. A marriage which made me feel trapped and suffocated. My sleep began to trouble me too. I would often experience episodes of sleep paralysis. During these episodes, my body became paralysed whilst sleeping and I was unable to scream out loud or call out for help. I would feel as though I was at the mercy of something dark and unpleasant which had a hold over me. The episodes would often last a few minutes, after which I would eventually regain the ability to move. These were no ordinary nightmares and I often wondered to myself whether they reflected my emotional state or perhaps it really was a dark entity smothering me. The truth of which, perhaps I will never know.

CHAPTER 7

Many a time my mind would recall the wonderful times I shared with Johan at university. In contrast to Sameer, he had been so caring and loving towards me. I remembered that, whenever we fought, he would very sweetly come to me to reconcile and make up. He would never allow an argument to go on for even more than a day. In fact, they barely lasted a few hours, if that. He was mature in many ways. He understood what being a partner meant. He wouldn't criticise me or make comments to hurt me. He accepted me for who I was and took the good with the bad. I began to question whether the love I had received from Johan was the only true love I would ever experience in my lifetime. At this time, I desperately wanted to contact Johan. Although I no longer desired to be with him, I missed our friendship. He understood my temper and my flaws and still saw the goodness in me, which helped to ground me. I missed the feeling of being understood and I missed being respected. The strange thing was, as kind as Johan was, I had always known in my heart that my relationship with Johan was not going to be forever. I had always felt that this relationship would only be for a season and that he would not be the man I would marry and be my 'happy ever after'. Neither was Sameer, and yet I had still married him.

In February 2008, I qualified as a lawyer and landed an amazing job with an American advertising giant. They wanted me to live in New York for a year and work out of their office in Madison Avenue. I declined the offer because I didn't want to leave Sameer behind. On some level, I guess I knew that, had I made the decision to move out to New York for a year, then I probably would have got a taste for freedom and what it felt like to be respected. I knew that I would have become highly susceptible to jumping ship and bailing out of the marriage. If I never allowed that to happen, I could foolishly pride myself on being a loyal and committed wife to Sameer. I therefore requested to work out of the New York office for just two months, rather than a year.

A city made vibrant by its eclectic mix of people and urban skyscrapers towering above, everyone seemed to be in a rush to go someplace and get something done. The energy in the city was exciting, addictive and sometimes a little frightening too, but it didn't stop me from exploring what it had to offer.

A few of my American colleagues would flirt outrageously with me and give me the come on. One was called Rob. He was of American-Irish descent and had an endearing New York Queen's accent which would make me laugh every time he would speak. He was a couple of years younger than me, but absolutely fixated with my British accent and would keep asking me to speak and repeat certain words. I enjoyed his attention. It had been a while since anyone had flirted with me so outrageously and although I wasn't looking to take things any further with him, he made me feel attractive and desirable once again. Rob had married just a few months earlier – however, that didn't seem to stop him searching incessantly for his next sexual conquest. He was cute and charming, and I could see why women fell prey to his flattery – however, I wasn't one of them.

I went out one evening with my team for a work social. By the time we got there, a lot of our work colleagues were extremely drunk. Married men and women were kissing and being intimate with each other in the far corners of the room, with little care in the world about who was watching. Some of them were a scotch away from getting a room for the night for a quick sexual hook-up. It was an eye opener for me and my colleague RJ who, like me, was starting to feel uncomfortable watching our senior colleagues acting with drunken abandon. RJ signalled at me for us to sneak out and go somewhere else. I was relieved, as it wasn't turning out to be my idea of an evening well spent either. RJ was originally from San Francisco. A quirky and intelligent man of South Korean descent. I think, deep down inside, that we were both a little taken back by how all these married men and women were cheating on their partners with their work colleagues, and how they seemed happy to jeopardise their marriages for just a quick drunken fumble, and potentially throw away anything good they may have had back at home. I then thought that perhaps some of them were not happy in their marriages and this was their escape or their release – their chance to go out and look for happiness. I, on the other hand, hid behind a pathetic veil of loyalty and commitment, which shamefully made me think that I was morally better than my counterparts.

The problem with sitting on a moral high horse at the cost of your own happiness, is that years pass you by in the blink of an eye. Then, in the end, all you are left with is hindsight and the opportunities that you let slip by, especially the ones that could have made you happy. I don't think cheating on Sameer would have been such an opportunity, nor do I think it would have made me happy, but I do regret the chances that I didn't embrace out of fear of losing a marriage that was never worth saving. I desperately wanted my marriage to work, and at all costs too. Regardless of Sameer's treatment of me, I was still committed to him, so much so that I would avoid dressing even in any remotely suggestive way. I preferred to dress modestly in order to avoid any blatant attention from other men. I'm not sure that he deserved this commitment and loyalty – however, I had always promised myself that I would tell my partner that the relationship was over before starting another relationship elsewhere. And so I stuck to this commitment, perhaps more for myself than for him. Once I returned to England, RJ and I stayed in touch over social media. He had a nice and gentle demeanour about him, and it reminded me how I missed having that calm, fun, male energy around me as I had done when I was younger and not married.

Once I returned to the London office, my boss Stuart started to make my life very difficult. Stuart was a forty-seven-year-old functioning alcoholic. His face bore deep lines and wrinkles which made him look far older than his years. His personality was reflected by his looks – a haggard, miserable old drunk. His face mirrored the mess that was within. Happy hour started every day for him at 6pm sharp, and if the team from New York were in town, it would start even earlier under the guise of after-work drinks. Being an advertising company, the business happily picked up the tab whilst its employees partied hard at its expense. Somehow, it was almost encouraged as being a part of the culture of the advertising world.

Stuart was in his element during such times as these, as he would indulge in a hedonistic and simultaneous cocktail of prostitutes, alcohol and cocaine. In the evenings, his larger-than-life ego would come out to play and party hard, and as the chemical high would wear off the following morning, his irritability would set in, revealing his true self to his colleagues. My American boss, Steve, was fond of me and appreciated what I brought to my role and to the company. He was quite keen to push me forward and wanted me to shine in front of other senior colleagues in our offices across the world. He wanted me to address the international CFOs and CEOs in a presentation at our company's world conference, which was to be held in Prague. I worked consistently hard on that presentation for two months straight, as I wanted to make sure it was perfect in every way possible. Stuart, however, felt threatened by this and didn't want me to rub shoulders with people that mattered in the company. He didn't want me to attend the conference in Prague and so he cancelled my trip at the last minute and told me that my presence would no longer be required there. Instead, he would now give the presentation to the delegates at the conference that I had prepared and worked so hard on. Naturally, this was a huge blow to my self-confidence. I became increasingly stressed at work and my heightened levels of anxiety meant that I couldn't sleep well at night. To make matters worse, Sameer wasn't being supportive either. Instead, he chose to argue with me, play on my insecurities and make my life more difficult than it already was, rather than support and comfort me. In the end I decided to resign from my job because the stress was taking a toll on my health. It wasn't the ideal time to take such a drastic step, as the UK markets had begun to crash, and the economy was in a steep decline. In the months that lay ahead, I struggled to find another job as the economy came to a standstill.

CHAPTER 8

Shortly after my 30th birthday, I discovered I was pregnant. I was beyond happy and filled with so much gratitude that God had answered my prayers. The timing wasn't ideal, as the economy was still a mess, and I still hadn't found a job. I had always wanted to be a mother and couldn't imagine my life without having experienced motherhood, and so I fully embraced this blessing with all my heart. I intuitively knew that my baby was a boy. I could feel it. My pregnancy, overall, was fine. However, during the first trimester the morning sickness was horrendous and quite upsetting at times.

During this time, my relationship with Sameer was more than strained, but not at its entire worst. There were a few instances where we argued. I had pregnancy hormones running riot throughout my body and at certain times I was overly sensitive and stubborn. One evening, Sameer yelled at me and got me really upset. I went for a drive in my car to get some head space and clarity. I decided to call Sameer to try and resolve our differences, but he carried on screaming and swearing at me. I had a panic attack and began to hyperventilate. Sameer would quite often get me into this state. I had to call the paramedics to help me calm down, as the panic was so severe. I was parked in a supermarket car park and I just couldn't seem to regulate my breathing. I was worried about the effect this would be having on my unborn baby. They arrived and calmed me down. Me and baby were fine. However, that night I decided to go to my parents and sleep there instead, as I needed some mental and physical respite. I didn't have sleep paralysis that night, but I could hear doors being slammed shut throughout the night and it kept waking me up. It was as if there was something in the house that was trying to get my attention. I tried to go back to sleep as I was too scared to get up and see what it was. I never did mention this to anyone, and the experience was left unspoken about.

In the Face of All Things Unknown

Come July, it was a hot summer morning, and I wasn't feeling too well. My swelling was extremely bad, and I had a rash everywhere which was making me really uncomfortable. At this point I was around 41 weeks pregnant. Even though Sameer had been yelling at me only days earlier, on this day he seemed a little calmer and insisted on taking me to the hospital. As we reached the maternity ward, the panic started. My baby was in distress, his heartbeat was extremely low, dangerously low. The midwives were shouting across to each other and panicking. I was rushed to the operating theatre for an emergency C-section. I was told that I had to be kept awake and conscious for the delivery and that they would numb the lower half of my body using a spinal block. However, it turned out that I was one of the few unfortunate ones, as the spinal block didn't work on me. I was one of those rare cases where this happened. As they tried to pull the baby out, I could feel everything that they were doing, and I was in agony. It was all too much, and I felt for a few moments that my end might be near. I started to pray intently as the pain became increasingly unbearable. I wanted to survive the surgery and live to see my child. By the grace of God, Zen was delivered safely weighing just 4lbs and 10 ounces. Although he was severely underweight at forty-one weeks old, he was otherwise fit and healthy in every other way. When they handed Zen over to me and put him in my arms, it was the most precious moment of my life. He was crying, but as soon as I looked at him and said, "Hello baby", he knew it was his mother's voice speaking to him. He immediately fell sleep in my arms, soothed and comforted by being close to me. Very quickly I became so aware of the powerful role that I would play in my little angel's life. Not only would I protect him with my life, but I would also be his nurturer, his teacher and possibly many other things in between.

A few hours later, as I awakened, the midwife who had first attended me when I arrived at the hospital came to visit me. As she enquired about my health, I noticed that she was overwhelmed with emotion and her eyes looked teary. She went on to tell me that had I not come into the hospital earlier that day when I did, then both baby and I could have died. Our medical complications had not been detected by the doctors earlier on in the pregnancy, and had they paid closer attention, then they would have realised that I had developed pre-eclampsia, a dangerous pregnancy condition. I was already traumatised by the earlier events of the day but hearing this made my head spin.

It was in fact Sameer who had insisted that I go to the hospital immediately that morning, as I had complained of not feeling too well and the swelling throughout my body was beyond the point of ridiculous. I would happily have waited and gone to the hospital after lunch. However, Sameer had insisted that

In the Face of All Things Unknown

I go to the hospital straightaway. It was Sameer's decisiveness that saved both of our lives that day. Had he not insisted, my son and I could have died.

They decided to keep me under close observation at the hospital, and so I was kept in the recovery unit for an additional night rather than being transferred to the maternity ward. The doctors were concerned that I may start to have fits and develop eclampsia. This can be life-threatening, as it carries the risk of seizures and coma, but fortunately that never happened, and I was transferred to the maternity ward the following day. Both of our respective families were all very happy that day. I wanted to cherish these magical moments with them all around me and my little angel. However, it wasn't long before Sameer and his mum broke into an argument beside my hospital bed, and neither one of them was willing to back down or shut up. My heart sank, because they had selfishly tainted this magical time with their usual toxic behaviour. They had no concern for my feelings or my health. The fact that I had just gone through a traumatic delivery and had extremely high blood-pressure seemed to mean nothing to them. They were far too engrossed in playing out their usual ego-based mind games and arguments to show any consideration for me and my new-born baby. This is how they welcomed my sweet little child into this world. My heart sank. There was no magical moment with Sameer, nor a kiss from him to say thank you or well done, or a "Look, that's our son". He simply went home to sleep, along with the rest of the family.

I was now alone with my baby and it was our first quiet moment together. The heavenly gift that I had prayed so hard for was now finally in my arms. He was perfect in every way possible. I remember an overwhelming feeling of guilt came over me. "Why had I brought something so beautiful and innocent into such a corrupt and mean world?" My heart was so heavy. How would I protect him from the arguments at home, and the explosive arguments that Sameer would have with his mother?

In the Face of All Things Unknown

CHAPTER 9

I was one of those loved-up mums who relishes every single minute of being with her baby. In fact, I hated being away from Zen. Sometimes I wondered whether Sameer was jealous of my love for Zen, as he would often try to find faults in my parenting. He would quite often ask me whether I loved Zen more than him. As a parent, this question never made any sense to me and it troubled me deeply. His increasing contempt for me would play out in many ways. He would shout, yell and swear at me on most days. On one evening, I remember asking Sameer to pick up some nappies for Zen from the supermarket. He of course didn't want to go, nor did he want to be bogged down with any extra responsibilities (not even for his new-born son), so he decided to take off somewhere in his car instead. Whilst driving off he stuck his two fingers up at me and shouted, "Fuck you" through the car window. He had become so spiteful and vengeful, and I didn't know where it was coming from. It was as though something had come over him so that he now despised me to my core. He wanted to yell at me at any given opportunity. He knew I was vulnerable and weak at this time and still healing from my surgery, but he used this time to slowly break my will. It began to break my heart too. He had no tenderness or care for me or Zen at this time. Sometimes when he would be screaming at me, I would have nowhere to go and so I would lock myself with Zen in his room and sing lullabies to him, to soothe and distract him and make him smile. There was nothing else I felt I could do at that time to protect myself, and I felt ashamed to tell my parents that this was how he was behaving with me.

During this time, I would often speak to my nani when I was alone. I always felt that she was still around me in spirit. I would often ask for her guidance and support, as I was at a loss as to what to do. I recall clearly feeling so jittery and anxious all the time, as though my head and heart were about to explode. Being stuck in a car with Sameer when he would become enraged was like being held in a hostage situation. He would drive recklessly when Zen and I were in the car with him. I would beg Sameer to slow down, but he would deliberately accelerate to well over ninety miles per hour and drive faster, swerving dangerously between the lanes in the road. My only comfort and solace whilst living in hell was being with Zen. He was where I found my peace. My beautiful baby was my godsend and was my little angel. In the months that followed, I immersed myself in the joys of motherhood and I loved every precious moment of it.

Meanwhile, my marriage was non-existent. We even slept in separate rooms. I didn't feel safe with Sameer anymore. He had become so volatile and uncontrollable that my time away from him at night was the only emotional respite I could get, to recharge and mend my frayed nerves. When Zen was six months old, Sameer managed to secure a well-paid job in Madrid, but they fired him after only a few weeks. I never did find out what happened in the end, and why they terminated his employment so abruptly. When he was at home, he was never interested in helping around the house. Sometimes just the mere suggestion of it would send him into a rage. It was easier not to ask anything of him unless it was absolutely necessary. That way I felt less anxious, as I thought it may help to avoid a showdown of any kind. Sameer's behaviour started to deteriorate even further. He often claimed he was depressed and so I tried my utmost to be patient with him. I often wondered if it was just depression, or something more, which would cause him to lash out at me over the smallest of things. He went through phases of sleeping for hours on end and some days would wake up in the early hours of the afternoon. I knew this wasn't normal, but the times when he was asleep were the only moments when I could enjoy peace and quiet at home. At all other times, being in the same space as him was like a match being continuously swiped along the edge of a matchbox. Any friction had the potential to spark a fire between us. I had always been told by people that I was a strong and determined person, but whilst living with Sameer I had wasted that strength in enduring a bitter and broken marriage. Had the same strength and determination been channelled elsewhere and more productively, perhaps I would have achieved more. Still, I clung on. I was desperate to find a cure for Sameer, because I still wasn't ready to give up nor believe and accept that he was responsible for his own behaviour. However, one thing that I did recognise was that his frequent bouts of binge drinking whilst taking anti-depressants were causing him to crumble even further. I tried to discuss this with him, but he was adamant that he knew exactly what he was doing and that I wasn't to interfere.

CHAPTER 10

With nowhere to turn, I began praying even more keenly for a happy and peaceful home. I felt that I needed to try and change myself so that my home environment would improve from a change of energy. I began reading as much as I could about connecting with God and exploring different aspects of spirituality. As my spiritual journey unfolded, I came to realise that I too could have been a better partner in our marriage. I realised that I didn't love fully nor with an open heart. Rather than offering my love without expectation, I would often look to see what Sameer was giving me in exchange. I tried to change myself and embrace a purer form of love, where I would try and show more patience and understanding towards him. I felt that rather than punishing him for being a wounded and hurting soul, I could heal him with love and compassion. For the next few months, I tried to be really loving and supportive of him. I would prepare freshly cooked meals for him and I tried to be more encouraging of his work and not critical. It didn't work. There wasn't any appreciation or acknowledgement of the effort I had been making. Instead, Sameer became increasingly demanding and cruel in his treatment of me. That's when I knew in my heart that nothing could make this marriage work. Sameer took for granted me and all my worth, and now nothing more could be done to fix it. I always knew deep down in my heart that the marriage was doomed to fail but I had refused to accept it. Until now. Sameer was on this high-speed train derailing towards self-destruction. I felt like I was also being dragged alongside him on this journey, except I didn't want to self-implode. I so desperately wanted to jump off this train, but I didn't know how. All I could see was danger ahead of me. It made me hesitant, and my fear paralysed me into a state of inertia.

I started to experience episodes of depression coupled with anxiety which would last a few days. I would want to lock myself in my room, curl up in a ball and hide from the world. At times, my chest would feel so tight that I wasn't able to breathe. I would be gasping for air, fearing the worst. I felt as though I was drowning in the negativity inside my mind. It felt so terrible, but it was also in that dark space that I would experience snatches of enlightening thoughts showing me where I had gone wrong in my life. It was often a time for me to tune into my intuition. The sound of my inner voice, that I had muted for years, now needed to be heard by me. I realised that I had suppressed my soul from expressing its true self and blossoming into that flower that it was always meant to be. Instead, I had developed a warped sense of self that was based on what others expected me to be. I had tried so very hard to fit that mould until I gave up. No matter how hard I tried, I was never going to be the perfect fit for someone else's expectations. How I longed to have the purity of expression and authenticity of a small child again, and express my likes, dislikes, needs, wants, and fears without the concern of being judged by others.

As I grew older, I learnt to wear several masks to conceal who I truly was. As a result, I began to project the image that I thought people wanted to see. Eventually I got tired. The lies and the false pretence caught up with me, manifesting itself in the form of depression. Although I would often dread this ghastly visitor, my brief encounters of depression would often bring with them the gift of 'spiritual revelation 'or 'spiritual awakening', where everything in my life was 'called for questioning'. It was at this time that I found myself looking within for the answers. I had a desperate need to eliminate those things in my life that no longer served me, or where radical change was needed for me to feel heard. Often this culminated in me having to state my boundaries to feel happier and more peaceful within. I soon realised that depression could quite often be a blessing in disguise for me, so long as I was ready to embrace this call to change and shake up my life and give it the much-needed overhaul that it so desperately required.

CHAPTER 11

Dad's best friend died suddenly in August. We were very close to Uncle Harish, who was pretty much like a father figure to Mina and I, and had been in our lives from the day we were born. Understandably, his death hit us hard. Sameer was in fact generally quite supportive around this time, but a day before uncle Harish's funeral, I was naturally feeling incredibly low and anxious about the occasion. I was extremely irritable and snappy and just needed to be left alone to manage my own feelings. Sameer couldn't understand my irritability at this time. All I needed was a comforting hug from him and for him to look past my current mood and snappiness, but instead he retorted with, "You fuckin' bitch, you're not the only one that's struggling right now." His comment hurt me in a way that I didn't even think was possible. That night, I could barely sleep. I kept thinking that if Sameer couldn't be there for me at a time such as this, then he would never be there for me in any capacity. I knew he would just kick me further when I felt down. He was devoid of any genuine empathy, care or respect for me, even in grief. That night, the pain that I felt in the depths of my soul, was crushing. It was as though every part of me had now shattered. I struggled to fall asleep, as I kept thinking repeatedly, how was he capable of such mental and emotional cruelty towards me.

I eventually fell asleep, but it was on this very night that I experienced my first out-of-body experience. It felt as though my soul was trying to leave my body. I was semi-conscious and could see my soul rising up about five or six inches above me, and this made me so fearful that I began praying. My soul then stopped, and then I saw a blue floating orb emerge out of my body. The orb was a beautiful electric blue in colour, and it had the face of a small boy inside of it. The boy smiled at me as the orb floated away and then disappeared.

I woke up the following morning to get ready for the funeral, but deep down inside I was baffled by what I had experienced the night before. I couldn't make any sense of it. It was as though I was being delivered a message of some sort, but I wasn't quite sure what it was. It was all a little unsettling because I knew that this experience was quite random and extremely rare. I didn't know anyone who had spoken about experiencing anything like this. A few days later, I consulted a friend of mine who happened to be a psychic. It turned out that she had never in all her twenty-five years of giving readings ever come across anything like this, but one thing that we both agreed on was that I was being delivered a message from beyond this realm. It seemed to me as though the orb was a supernatural guide or angel of some sort, but what was this message that they were trying to tell me, other than reassure me with their presence?

A few weeks passed and my birthday was fast approaching. Somehow, intuitively, I just knew that this birthday was going to be a pivotal time in my life. I had this knowing feeling that one way or another my fate was about to be decided once and for all. I began to pray for a miracle. Every day leading up to my birthday I would ask God and my guardian angel to show me a sign and guide me as to what to do. I was lost and could not see a way out. I needed their help as I was devoid of courage and at a point in my life where I didn't have the income to help me raise my son and provide a roof over our heads. My self-respect and confidence were at an all-time low, and the fleeting episodes of depression were becoming increasingly more and more common.

Ashamed of what I had become, I would often hide my true self from my family and friends. I couldn't face seeing the disappointment in their eyes every time they would look at my sorry state and at how I was living. They knew that I would manufacture excuse after excuse to avoid family gatherings and social events. I was now hiding my miserable and overweight self, whilst fighting a constant fatigue, trying to survive one crisis after another. I was broken. I prayed for a way out of this painful existence where my soul was tortured every second of every day. I wanted to escape this marriage which I had to admit to myself had never been a marriage in the true sense of the word. Instead, it was a battleground, that forced me to rise from the dead every single morning, only to face yet another death, every single day. My prayers became more frequent and fervent, as I would ask God to grant me the strength and the wisdom to have clarity of mind and make the best decisions for Zen and me. I felt crushed by the pain of my circumstances and was fearful because I couldn't see a way out. I felt obliged to stay in my marriage and to keep trying to make it work, at least for the sake of my little Zen. The hard truth though, on every level, was that this marriage was wrong. I was fearful that Sameer would make our lives even more unbearable, and I no longer had the strength to go on. I felt trapped by my circumstances, and so I asked God to bring the right people into my life to help show me the way so that I could eventually take Zen and myself out of this mess. I prayed every night for this miracle.

CHAPTER 12

Ever since I was a child, I loved travelling and wanted nothing more than to explore the world. Travelling was my heart's song, and this was where I was completely in my element. I decided to book Sameer, Zen and me a short break to the beautiful city of Istanbul. A change of scenery was much needed at this time, as the last couple of months had been particularly heavy and draining for us, especially since my uncle's sudden death. Throughout the trip, Sameer's behaviour was even more erratic than usual. He told me that the doctor had prescribed him stronger anti-depressants to help regulate his mood. However, throughout the trip, Sameer wouldn't stop drinking. He would tag along to all the excursions that I had booked, but he would just sleep throughout the coach trips that we made, leaving Zen and me to carry on between ourselves, as though he wasn't there with us. The entire time, Sameer drank constantly and without thought.

On our last evening in Istanbul, I was in the hotel room packing our suitcases for the return journey home. It was only 7pm and Sameer was already unusually drunk for this time. He was particularly worked up about something and only God knows what was going through his head that day, as he wouldn't stop abusing me verbally. Sameer was relentless and he wouldn't stop coming after me. He followed me into the bathroom and cornered me. He put his face against mine and forced me to hear all the hurtful things that he wanted to say about me. I asked him to stop. I begged and I pleaded but he wouldn't listen. When the taxi arrived to take us to the airport, Sameer was almost comatose as he was so drunk, and then suddenly he was violently sick all over the taxi. As the taxi pulled into the departures drop-off point, the driver of course wanted to be compensated with 500 Turkish lira so that he could get the taxi professionally cleaned. Sameer was outraged by this and started screaming at the taxi driver. The police were alerted to the disturbance and a team of six Turkish police officers walked over to intervene. When he was asked to quieten down, Sameer wouldn't have any of it and instead he started to scream back at the police officers. They threatened to arrest him, but even then, Sameer wouldn't shut up. Poor Zen saw it all. He was visibly shaken up by his father's behaviour and did not understand why Daddy was behaving this way. He was seven years old, and I could no longer lie to him about what was going on. His eyes could not lie to him either, as the truth was there, right in front of him. It was the most humiliating day of my life. Surprisingly, the police allowed Sameer to catch the flight and travel back home with us. It was only a four-hour flight, but it was the longest journey of my life.

Sameer had now completed his metamorphosis into a monster that had lost all sense of control. He no longer cared about his surroundings nor what people thought of him anymore. When we reached home that evening, I couldn't get to sleep and so I started to pack my bags. The following morning, with Zen, I left that house for good.

CHAPTER 13

Zen and I returned to my parents' home. We had nowhere else to go. I had a part-time job at a local insurance company, that barely paid my bills. I was far from being in a position where I could rent my own place. I had some savings, but if I had moved out into a rented studio apartment, my savings would have evaporated within five or six months. Christmas was tough. I felt low, ashamed, and sad. Nothing in life felt good anymore. At times, I didn't even want to be alive. I was thirty-eight-years-old, and every aspect of my life seemed a failure. My career had failed, my marriage had failed and, most of all, I felt like I had failed at life. This was not the life I had etched out for myself and dreamt as a child of living. I didn't recognise who or what I had become anymore because the current 'me' was not the true reflection of who I really was deep down. I feared that the real me would never surface nor would my soul ever get to express its true essence. I worried my life would pass before my eyes with all my dreams left unfulfilled. This was not the trajectory I was meant to be on. I had spent so many years training to be a lawyer, and yet today I had no confidence to even apply for a job that I was worthy of. I lacked confidence in my own abilities, but most of all, I lacked self-worth. I had not mapped out this life for myself. How on earth had I ended up here? In the months that followed, I hardly left my parents' home. Being awake and facing people was hard work. It required more energy and strength than I had within me. I just wanted to sleep. Being surrounded by people gave me anxiety. I just wanted to be left alone. Those closest to me would often tell me to "pull myself together", except it wasn't as easy as that. Inside, I felt broken. Inside, I was lost.

It was finally happening – I was getting divorced, and this was uncharted waters for me. There was a huge sense of grief for the marriage that I never had and the dream that was unfulfilled. There was the feeling of shame for having failed at something so important, and anger for the years that had been wasted in the desperate and futile pursuit of saving something that had never really been worthy of being saved. The news of my divorce quickly reached many ears. My internal, ugly, dark life had been exposed to the world and now the vultures kept coming to enjoy their feast. They would feast on my misery and they feasted on my pain. That winter was long. The darkness outside also loomed inside my mind. Life was too painful to live, and I didn't know how to numb the anguish and the pain and that nagging, destructive voice in my mind that was forcing me down a long descent. It would have been all too easy at that time to reach for anything to help numb the pain, but I feared for my son. I might have failed at life, but I didn't want to fail my little boy. He deserved better from me. My beautiful little Zen deserved to have me at my best, but I didn't know how to be that way for him. My heart felt scared, and my mind seemed uncertain.

As Christmas and New Year celebrations passed, I began to truly struggle as I reflected upon my life. I felt as though I was in the deepest depths of depression – however, unlike all the other times when I had felt depressed, this time there wasn't even a tiny glimmer of hope left. Only darkness surrounded me. It was hard to be around people. Even my loved ones and, shockingly, even Zen. It required a lot from me. A lot of energy that I no longer had. I didn't feel normal or happy within myself. Throughout my past struggles, there had always been a glimmer of hope that pulled me through the darkest of days, but now even that flame was out.

I spent many long hours crying into my pillow. I felt shame and I felt guilt but most of all I felt as though my heart had been ripped out of my body. I wished to be still, and numb the despair that was too deep. I wasn't sure how I was going to raise my son with such a low-paid job and broken confidence. I felt trapped by my failures, by my fears and my own shortcomings, and most of all by the web of my own misfortune. That was perhaps the longest and darkest winter of my life.

Right now, I only had two options. To either listen to that ugly self-critical and destructive voice in my mind or, instead, surrender my fears to God and to be guided by His divine light. I chose the latter. I began praying to God and my angels to help me and show me the way. I prayed for a sign and most of all I prayed for a miracle. I now needed divine guidance to pull me out of this dark place because I couldn't do this anymore and I wasn't sure if I had the will to go on. I knew I could no longer hide from myself. I was now ready to heal from within, and so I surrendered my pain to them.

CHAPTER 14

It was 4am. I had been woken from my sleep by an alarming sound. It was the sound of what seemed like large beating wings. I kept hearing it, and each time I rose from my bed to see what it was. I could see nothing and would return to sleep, only to be woken up, time and time again, by the same sound, except no culprit was to be found. My intuition led me to believe that it was my guardian angel making me aware of their presence and letting me know that I wasn't alone. I was protected. Perhaps this was the sign I had been praying for all along and now I just had to have faith in God's plan for me.

The following morning, I woke up feeling as though my head was in a fog. I slowly got dressed and left the house for work. It was a bitterly cold morning, and my thick quilted coat was barely keeping me warm during my long walk to the station. Fortunately, just as I was coming down the stairs, there was a Central Line tube approaching the platform. The train was packed full of people already, and as I weaved my way through them, I found a small gap and decided to park myself there until I reached my destination. As the train went along and collected more and more passengers from each stop, I began to feel uneasy. It was as though the world was closing in on me, and my head began to spin. The train came to a halt as it reached White City station. However, in my mind, the train felt like it was sliding backwards and so I started to panic, thinking we were about to crash. In sheer panic, and fearing the worst, I let out a loud scream, "It's moving backwards, stop the train!" The last thing I remember was that everything began spinning and whirling around me.

When I opened my eyes, I didn't recognise where I was. I tried to lift my head to take a better look but, oh my God, the splitting pain in my head was excruciating, as I seemed to have fallen over and banged it. I was almost in tears, until a gentle voice came over and slowly whispered in my ear, "It's okay, just relax, you're safe with me, I've got you". I couldn't see his face as I could barely open my eyes, but I could feel the tenderness in his touch, as he stroked my head and then held my hand. I then fell into a deep sleep until the following morning. When I opened my eyes, I could see this same beautiful looking man, asleep in the chair at the foot of my bed. I was immediately drawn to his mild face which looked so peaceful and serene as he slept.

Careful not to wake him from his sleep, I slowly reached for the glass of water which was on the table beside me. In the strangely excited yet anxious mess that I was in, I managed to knock this over and with this he woke up immediately and was somewhat startled. As my eyes met his, I think time happened to stand still. He seemed to have a look of surprise upon his face. I was paralysed by his perfect smile and his beautiful yet gentle eyes. "I guess we finally meet", he said. "I'm Krish. Perhaps you don't remember, but you passed out and collapsed on the Tube. You knocked your head as you fell, and you were unconscious for some time. I came with you in the ambulance to the hospital." "It's strange, but I can't seem to recall what happened", I replied. "'Krish', that's a very Indian-sounding name, except you don't look very Indian." "It's short for Krishna", he said. "My 'Indian-ness' is hardwired into my DNA alongside the other 50%, which is Italian, thanks to my father." This finely blended cocktail of genes explained his perfect and yet mysterious looks. He had very gentle eyes. They were innocent and yet mischievous all at once. In fact, I couldn't stop staring at them and his beautiful face. This was so unlike me, as I found nothing more uncomfortable than holding my gaze whilst talking to someone. It was nothing short of awkward. There was no hiding the intense magnetism that existed between us. It was as though we were both in tune with one another and on the same frequency. We were interrupted by a firm knock at the door. It was the nurse, doing her rounds of the patients on the ward and checking to see that their vital signs were all okay. "You're incredibly lucky, you know. There are not many people out there that would stay by the side of a stranger for a whole twenty-four hours, the way this young gentleman did with you. He was worried that if he left, you would wake up alone and quite possibly panic or feel scared."

As the nurse left and Krish turned to me, I could see he felt a little awkward and somewhat embarrassed. Quickly changing the subject, he said, "You must be hungry, so have this. I picked you up a pasta salad from the canteen downstairs. You can't really go wrong with pasta. It's usually a safe bet." He smiled. My right arm and hand were still extremely bruised from my fall the day before. I was struggling to hold the fork in my hand as I attempted to eat my lunch. Krish noticed this and said, "Hey, let me help with you that". He took the fork right out of my hand and began feeding me. It didn't feel awkward being fed by a complete stranger. Rather, it felt quite natural. I felt very safe with him. His energy was so calm and nurturing. In fact, it was so unlike anything I was used to. I was used to being yelled at whenever I was sick or ill. Being out of action for a few days had always been deemed a hindrance to Sameer's lifestyle, because it meant that I was unable to provide a clean house, hot meals and handle the responsibility for Zen single-handedly. Thoughts of Zen started to make me panic. He was away on a residential school trip for the entire week in the Lake District. I was worried that Zen or his teacher may have tried to contact me whilst I had been unconscious. I sat upright and started gabbling at Krish. I asked whether I had any calls on my phone, and if my son was okay. Krish assured me that everything had been tended to by him. He had located the number of my friend Alison, on my phone, which he had found in my bag and informed her that I was in hospital. Alison then made the necessary calls to my family and Zen's school. I was not used to being treated so tenderly. Then, Krish could see my eyes were becoming heavy with sleep. He told me to get some rest and that he would return in the evening to check up on me. He tucked me snugly beneath the bedsheets and leant forward to kiss me on my forehead before he left. I did not want him to leave but felt a little embarrassed and almost greedy for wanting him to stay.

Over the next few days, Krish would come often to the hospital to check up on me. The fall had been triggered by severe dizziness and the doctors wanted to run multiple tests to make sure there wasn't anything else sinister going on with me. I felt safe having Krish there beside me. This was quite an unusual feeling for me because just days earlier I felt as though I was in the throes of the deepest depression. I usually did not like to be in the company of anyone for a prolonged period of time. It required a huge amount of effort on my part. However, I didn't feel this way around him. I felt I could be myself even in the vulnerable state that I was in. Nor did I feel the need to hide myself or the real me. I didn't feel ashamed. Perhaps that's what it was. For some unexplainable reason, I felt beautiful in his presence, despite being bare-faced and make-up free during my hospital stay. He made me feel beautiful both inside and out. Krish and I would often talk for hours when he would come to visit me at the hospital. We spoke about relationships and the abusive marriage that I had left behind, and we also spoke of God and how, if one still has hope, He will find a way, no matter what. The words and thoughts just flowed between us. The conversation felt effortless. At some point during my conversation with Krish, I realised that there was something beautiful about expressing my authentic self. Perhaps it is the closest that we get to see the soul for what it is and what it was always meant to be.

During my stay at the hospital, I felt as though I was living in a twilight zone. Nothing seemed real or normal. I kept waking from my sleep feeling drained, tired, and sweaty, as though my body had gone through an intense workout. In fact, it felt like my body and soul were going through a spiritual upgrade and were beginning to heal. I began to heal emotionally too. I felt happier and lighter and once again I felt that there was hope. The physical pain that I had had in my body for months prior to my fall, in my knees and my abdomen, also began to leave me. It was as though the load I had been carrying all these years was now slowly shifting, and all the hurt I had stored inside my body was now being released.

I began to experience thoughts of clarity. It was as though I could look at my life from afar and understand for myself where I had gone wrong in my life. I could only describe this phenomenon that I was experiencing as a series of spiritual downloads. I felt as though messages were being conveyed especially to me, for me to understand and take heed. The first message that I had been sent was about ego. The reason that I had chosen to put up with a damaging and difficult marriage for so long was due, in part, to my ego. When I first met Sameer, my ego thought that he would be a good partner for me. He was fun, he was energetic, outgoing, and well connected. These were all attributes that I wrongly perceived would make me look good in the eyes of the world. It was also my ego that held me back from admitting that I was failing at my marriage. My ego wouldn't allow me to suffer this personal failure, so I had to succeed at all costs, which meant that I stayed put. Projecting the image of 'being married and together' to the world was clearly more important to me than my own happiness. I now needed to right-size my ego, because making decisions from a place that purely served my ego was detrimental to my overall wellbeing, and it kept me away from reaching and realising the goals that I needed to achieve.

Every moment of every day, every inch of my body had known that that marriage was wrong, and yet I stayed. I gave that man the best years of my life – my youth. I would often feel so angry at my own stupidity for allowing that to happen to me. There was so much grief at those precious years of my life that I had lost and would never get back. Many years had passed living in that hell, and I had done that to myself. The second message that was sent to me was that "Marriage in the absence of divine love is just a contract". I was delivered this message because I had always struggled with the thought of divorcing Sameer. I had grown up thinking that all marriages are made in heaven and that somehow this was what God had intended for me. It was in some way fated and that is why I had to endure the pains of this marriage. I would often see my marriage with Sameer as punishment for some past life sin or karma, rather than a lesson that I had to learn and grow from. In fact, what I had needed to do all along was to understand myself and see what was keeping me stuck there in that unhappy space. All this was what I needed to unravel.

The final message that came to me was that I had to surrender my fear, my guilt and my insecurities to the universe and to God. As I began to do this, I started to recognise those faults of mine which had contributed to the failure of the marriage. I had to recognise that I too had hurt people along the way, including Sameer. I began to reflect upon past relationships where I hadn't treated people with the level of respect that they had deserved, or certain friendships that I had taken for granted. Everything in my timeline had slowly come up for scrutiny and inspection and so, as the days rolled on, I took stock, and I took heed from this divine guidance that was being given to me.

I would quite often share these 'spiritual downloads' with Krish. It felt as though he was the one person that would understand my mind and see right through my soul and not think that I was slowly losing my sanity. Krish showed great interest in my spiritual journey and would listen to me without making me feel judged. That is one of the things that made him so special to me – his acceptance of me, without judgement.

CHAPTER 15

I had experienced another episode of sleep paralysis during my stay at the hospital. My body was once again gripped with fear, as I tried to wake up but couldn't. My body felt numb, with only my mind being alert and awake. The ghost of an elderly English woman came before me. She appeared to be looking straight at me. She was dressed in a formal-looking black overcoat and hat that was reminiscent of 1940s' England. She was probably in her mid- to late-seventies and was of a heavy and rather plump build. I vividly recall that, upon seeing her face, I instinctively knew that it was the face of a ghost. I tried to wake up from the nightmare, but I just could not move. I was paralysed yet conscious. I then looked up at the ceiling and could see a dark, black shadow hovering above my head. This dark mass was emanating a feeling of negativity, heaviness, and fear. It tried to infiltrate my body and consume me. I was so frightened by this dark figure because I instinctively knew that I was in imminent danger. To ward off this malignant, dark energy, I began praying frantically. I kept repeating the mantra 'Om Namah Shivay' again and again, for protection. After a minute or so of determined chanting, the black, shadowy figure finally left me alone and went away.

As I woke up, frantic with fear, Krish happened to walk into my hospital room. I was so relieved to see his face. He immediately knew I was in distress and came over to hold and comfort me. "Are you OK, are you in pain?" he asked. I explained to Krish what had just happened to me and what I had just seen. However, he didn't seem alarmed or surprised. "I know", said Krish. "I could feel your distress and sense your fear too. That's why I came rushing back." I was a little confused by his comment and he recognised this. "I have what you may call a sixth sense. I can tune into the emotions of others and that is how I came to know what it is that you are feeling." Krish walked over to me and held me. It was as though he could feel my pain, my fear, my love, and my happiness, as though it was his. I didn't understand how this was at all possible. His touch was so tender and so soothing that when he held me, it felt like a knowing of our souls. I felt so safe, as though there was a feeling of coming home. Everything seemed so familiar, yet it was all so new. After years of unkindness, I found kindness and love in the arms of a stranger. Krish was an immediate source of comfort for me.

The scent of his body was so delicious that it made me want to pull him in even closer to me. I knew Krish could feel something too. He looked deep into my eyes and tenderly held my face with both hands. He reached down to kiss my lips and I kissed him back. At that point it felt like lightning had struck me and something happened in that moment that was unexplainable. The connection between us was so intense, it was as though we could feel and sense the other's thoughts and desires. The kiss lingered until we were interrupted by a knock at the door. It was the doctor, doing his final round of check-ups before I could be discharged from the hospital. Krish helped me gather my belongings. We both knew that we wanted more of the magic we had just tasted before we had been interrupted by the doctor. "Listen, why don't you come and stay with me for a few days whilst you're recovering and, that way, I can take better care of you." He said this with a faint smirk on his face. We both knew what type of "better care" he had in mind and so we both broke into laughter, as it was clear we were both thinking the same

thing. As we sat in the taxi on our journey back to his flat, I found myself reaching out to hold his hand. I lay my palm upon his. The electric spark was still very much there, except you just couldn't see it. We finally reached his house. He showed me around his immaculate place, and I immediately felt comfortable and at ease there. It had a nice vibe and energy to it. Then he led me to his bedroom. He passionately reached for my waist and pulled me closer into him. As he caressed and gently held my face, he reached for my lips and kissed me again. I could feel my body melt and surrender to his touch as he ran his fingers across my back. "Have I been here before?" I wondered. He led me to the bed where we lay in each other's arms. His warm embrace felt all too comforting. His eyes were so familiar, so deep, so kind and inviting, pulling me even closer into him. With an intense look of passion and desire in his eyes, we both knew that we wanted each other.

Somehow, I knew that my search had stopped with him, and if time could have stood still, I would have captured that moment with my beloved forever. Perhaps he was always meant to know me a little better than anyone else had before him; perhaps I had known him from a lifetime before. Who was he, what was he and why was this feeling so compelling that I never wanted to leave his side and be in the arms of another ever again? I hadn't simply fallen in love with him. Instead, this felt as if it was a realisation of the love that I had always had for him. I knew instinctively that he had come into my life to awaken me to the reality of the authentic me. Krish had appeared at a time when I wasn't even able to love myself. My life had reached a crisis point where I was broken and had lost all sense of who I was, and even the thought of loving another had seemed like an impossibility at that time. However, instead, as the days went on, I found myself loving more deeply and strongly and in a way that I had never done before. I had not thought that a love so deep was possible. There was an undeniable, overwhelming feeling that we had been brought together as part of a higher calling. It was as though our meeting had been precisely planned and had been years in the making. The exact timing of the crossing of our paths had been divinely orchestrated, as neither one of us was looking for love. It was as if, in this lifetime, our souls had chosen to meet and reunite once again.

Although we had only known each other for a matter of days, intuitively I knew that we had been brought together to love, grow and heal alongside one another. Over time, the comfort of this knowledge helped me to develop my higher self. With the help of Krish I also began to learn and understand how to embody divine love for myself. Something that I had never understood before. He began to make me believe in myself once again. He treated me with such love and tenderness and gave me so much respect, that it slowly began to heal me and restore the self confidence that I had lost whilst married to Sameer. Krish encouraged me to resume once again my career as a lawyer. I felt scared but protected by his love. He would pray every day for my happiness and success so that I could once again get a good job, which would allow me to take care of myself and Zen. This was how deep his affection and care were for me, and so I reluctantly began to apply for jobs that I had no longer felt worthy of holding. I was unconvinced that anyone would hire me but Krish had full faith in me and my abilities, and he would not let me give up on myself. Three months later, his prayers for me were answered as I once again resumed my career as an in-house lawyer within a large international recruitment company in London. Fortunately, this job paid me a generous salary, which meant that overnight the dreams that I had written off for me and Zen were now finally accessible and within my reach.

As the months went by, Krish and I had become so close that I almost felt a little embarrassed at how uninhibited I was around him and how I would just reel off what I was thinking and feeling in my heart and mind, giving little thought as to how he would react. For the first time in all my history of dating men, I found myself not worrying about scaring him off. I knew that this love would only be true for as long as I presented the real me to him, the authentic me, and the day that I stopped doing this would also be the end of this great love.

And so, I carried on being me. There were no secrets anymore. I had surrendered to him and to our love. I felt compelled to release any negative thoughts and insecurities along the way, and as I did, I would experience epiphanies which were necessary for my own healing. Just by being around him and expressing myself authentically, I felt as though he was mending my soul, bit by bit, piece by piece. Loving Krish came from a place so pure and untainted that my connection with him allowed me to be free and vulnerable. Until I met Krish, I had never allowed myself to be this way with anyone. It was as though he illuminated all the darkness within me and all the ugliness that had surfaced. I was frustrated at my life and my failures, but he still accepted me, despite my weaknesses, my insecurities, my shortcomings, and my anger. Krish would often tell me, "Fortune smiles upon those who have gratitude for life's offerings. When you do not love yourself, you find it difficult to love everything that is connected to you. So, learn to love yourself first, then you will once again fall in love with the world that you find yourself in." He would also remind me not to be led by the fears in my mind, and instead to listen to the voice of my heart. Krish often spoke in riddles. He would address any questions that I asked, but not by answering them directly or addressing my fears for our future together. Although his answers mostly made sense to me, they often left me confused and frustrated, which would then trigger me to look inwards for answers. Perhaps I was seeking answers from him that he did not have answers to either.

I often questioned the nature of our connection. What were we to one another? Why was this relationship so intense, so bewildering and the connection between us telepathic and so deep? Why had God made our paths cross at a time when I had lost all love for myself? And yet intuitively, upon meeting Krish, I had known immediately that I loved him. It was as though I had always loved him, perhaps even from a previous lifetime. It was never just a physical attraction between us – it was deep care, a love and a knowing that transcended anything that I had ever experienced before.

It was as though I had recognised his soul and it was this soul recognition that gave me comfort. He was like a beacon of bright, white, brilliant light illuminating the darkness within and reminding me how truly I was loved. He wasn't just a ray of hope, he was 'hope' itself, like a shining star in the vast, black landscape of the deepest skies, shielding my heart from the storms of my own mind. My strength lay in my surrender to Krish. I had found the divine in him. Despite all my flaws he still found me beautiful. Such was the strength of his love that it empowered me. It gave me wings to once again start doing the things I had stopped doing for myself and, most of all, his love gave me the courage to once again start dreaming, and not give up hope of having happiness in my life.

CHAPTER 16

With the divorce behind me, I was led by a strong conviction and belief that there would be divine retribution for all the pain that I had suffered. I wasn't quite sure how this would happen, but I knew that I had to surrender my pain to God and pray for my healing. Seeking revenge for what I had endured was not my business, nor my concern. I just focused on getting to a better place emotionally, physically and within my career. I started to do all the positive things that I could physically manage which would help me get to a better place. I began working out at the gym and taking pride

In the Face of All Things Unknown

in my appearance once again. I began eating much more consciously and carefully. I started to take care of myself in ways that I had not done before. I also threw myself into my career, to gain myself a secure financial footing, as I knew this job could take me onto much better things. As I looked back at photos of yesteryear, I saw that younger version of myself in her twenties. I remember at the time being riddled with so much self- doubt and self-hatred. My body wasn't good enough, my face wasn't pretty enough, my legs weren't long enough, and I hadn't reached those pinnacles of success that my friends were flying high on. The list was endless, and the plague of self-doubt was so deeply entrenched within me. I had been a pretty young girl who was intelligent and had every reason to select only that which would have been for her greatest good, but I hadn't!

The truth was, I had always been good enough and I was always beautiful, and yet I had failed to see that within myself. I had refused to believe it, and more than anyone, I now had to find forgiveness for myself, for all those bad decisions that I had made and which I had refused to resolve. I had to forgive myself for choosing my ego over love and lacking in care and respect for myself. I now knew that, going forward, I had to learn and grow from these harsh lessons that I had unconsciously chosen for myself.

CHAPTER 17

One morning, eighteen months or so after our divorce, I was tired of feeling consumed by the negative feelings that I was holding towards Sameer and for the apology that never came from him. I decided to pick up the phone and wish Sameer all the best in life. I'm not quite sure what came over me, but I had this overwhelming feeling that I no longer wanted to carry hatred for him. I wanted him to find his happiness and I wished him well in his healing. He was appreciative of my call and almost emotional too at my gesture. When you finally decide to lay down your weapons, you realise that anger is such hard work! Thereafter, everything started to feel quite different, almost as though some cords that had us tied, even subconsciously, had now been broken. My soul had forgiven him, and I was now free to leave my old life behind and step into the new. That is when I realised that we should honour our heart's higher calling, which is to love and not to hate, even if that means forgiving those whose hearts are filled with hate for you. If you carry hate, it seeps into your heart and into every inch of your body until it consumes you entirely and eats into who you are. All along, I had tried to fix him because I knew he was hurting.

I had tried to control his journey towards healing, out of fear. I wanted him to be in a better space for the marriage. I waited and I controlled, and I urged him to get help, until the resentment grew on both sides. Rather than trying to control and accelerate his journey towards healing, I realise now that I should have stepped back and 'held space' for him. I should have been present and prayed for his healing so that he could awaken and enable the inner healing within himself if he had wanted to. I should have walked away when I had realised that many years had passed, and Sameer still was not ready to face the inner turmoil within, and to heal himself. All I had control of was me. I needed to look inside of me and to heal me first and understand all the choices that I had made for myself that had led me to this juncture in time. My first duty was to myself to my soul, whose voice I had silenced.

CHAPTER 18

My mind often swayed between the short-lived bliss of complete and utter surrender to love, and fear. They say you can only ever choose one master, love or fear, and quite often my mind would flip and worship the latter. My fear would make me run, because as much as I loved Krish with such intensity, I was so scared of the feelings that started to occupy my mind. He had given me feelings of immense happiness and love, something that I had never experienced before, but rather than having gratitude for it, I kept finding myself in such an anxious and fearful state. I wasn't used to happiness in my life, nor was I used to love, and when Krish came along, I soon developed a constant fear that this love would not last forever, or that it couldn't possibly be mine or be here to stay. Perhaps I feared the uncertainty of tomorrow because Krish's love had given me such bliss and never had I been treated with such tenderness and care. I was scared to get used to this kind of love. It seemed so unfamiliar to me and I couldn't bear getting hurt again. I realised that my pain had caused a deep well within me which I had chosen to fill with fear and not love. I needed so desperately to stop my suffering! I needed to step outside of it but didn't quite know how. I kept reminding myself that everything I ever wanted in life was on the other side of my fears. I wanted Krish. My heart kept telling me that my search had stopped with him, and that he was what my heart had been in search of because I knew that I wouldn't know a purer love elsewhere. My heart would tell me that Krish's love for me was real and sincere, although my mind would tell me otherwise. God had given me a big heart with which to love, and I had a lot of love to give, but I had little courage to receive it. Soon the self-doubt, which had always affected every aspect of my life, began to surface. When faced with even the smallest of criticism or perceived threat, it would become much bigger in my mind and would trigger either a flight or fight response within me. There was no balance, as I often swung from one extreme to another. It's because I didn't feel safe and secure in life. I didn't feel grounded.

A few turbulent months had passed where both Krish and I were under extreme pressure. Sameer was being extremely hostile and aggressive every time he would spend time with Zen and bring him back home to me. He would use as many tactics as he could to desperately try and keep me under his reign of terror, even though we were no longer together. Krish was also at an extremely low point in his life. His career as a cinematographer had taken a drastic downturn and the projects that he had lined up seemed to have evaporated within weeks. He was struggling to make ends meet. My neediness for Krish at this time proved to be too much for him, as he himself was struggling with his own feelings of self-worth. I didn't understand what he was going through at the time and I felt disappointed and angry at him for not being there for me, as he had been before. My anger was coming from a place of vulnerability and sadness and not spite. It was more love and understanding that my heart needed at this time. Krish would try his best to calm me down even though he was struggling to keep afloat himself, but each time we didn't see eye to eye, my anger would get the better of me.

Despite Krish's best endeavours to pacify me and keep me at ease, I wouldn't listen, and I still felt insecure. He refused to argue with me, and as he was faced with little choice, he slowly began to pull away from me. The more clarification I sought, the more silent he became. I could feel myself panic. A sense of desperation overcame me. I began to question, why was he pulling away, did he not love me? Was I no longer attractive to him? Why wasn't he answering my calls the way he used to? Why was he not replying to me the way he used to? Was he playing games with me? And so the list went on and on and the questions in my mind would never end. Day by day my anxiety grew, and a sense of restlessness gripped my very core. I was beginning to lose my patience with him, and the increased sense of uncertainty made me very irritable and short with him. I had convinced myself that perhaps he'd had his fun with me and now I probably wasn't as attractive to him anymore. Perhaps he was looking for pastures new and another conquest. As my mind ran wild with endless thoughts, I managed to work myself into a frenzy. I convinced myself that his evasiveness was due to a specific female friend that he had become very close to in recent weeks. I questioned whether she was poisoning his mind against me, because his love for me seemed to have vanished in an instant. I felt jealous that another woman was now stepping into my shoes, and I was upset with Krish because his love for me seemed to have proved so fickle and he had now allowed this to happen between us. I argued with him and I probed him for answers.

He told me that nothing was going on between them and that, contrary to my accusations, he had in fact told this friend that I was special to him and that he loved me. I still didn't believe him, and I accused him of playing games with me and cheating on me.

A few days of silence between us passed. Perhaps it was even a week. Thoughts of doubt started to flood my mind. Had I been too quick in accusing Krish of cheating on me? Did he mean what he said, that nothing had happened between them and that they were only friends? I sent him a text apologising for my lack of belief in him. He called back immediately, and we spoke at length and agreed to try harder with our communication. I even suggested that we go abroad for a few days. He considered the idea, but he seemed cautious and unconvinced, almost a little distant.

Two days later, Krish got the news that a major project that he was banking on financially, had fallen through. There were now no more projects in the pipeline for him, and nor were his former clients paying him his due for work that he had carried out for them with great tenacity. I told him not to worry and to keep his vibration high, as something would work out. A few encouraging messages later, he still hadn't replied to me. This went on for a few days and then the days turned into weeks. He still wouldn't reply to my texts or my calls. I would be lucky if I would receive a line or two, where he would thank me for my concern, and remind me that he wasn't in the space to be in touch with me or anyone. His posts on social media told me a different story. He looked happy. He was smiling and was socialising as usual. He seemed happy being around his friends, who were mostly female. However, I seemed to be the only idiot that he wasn't in the space to be in touch with.

I now started to feel increasingly angry at Krish and then at myself. I began to question his love for me. I questioned my own stupidity. I felt as though I had been preyed upon and that my heart had been toyed with when I was at my most vulnerable in life and was already on my knees. How did I manage to get it so wrong once again? How did God allow this to happen to me when I was just starting to heal from having been broken and damaged? And what about the feelings of divine love that he had evoked within me? Was that just my imagination? Had I dreamt this all up, like some make-believe fantasy? My head would spin frantically as I tried to grasp what had happened between us, and how this seemingly perfect love between us had just disappeared as if it had never even existed. I remember that day so clearly. I had been sobbing into my pillow until the early hours of the morning. I barely got three hours sleep that night and had to wake up early the following day. As I drove into work that morning, I realised that it was okay to fight for someone you loved but it was not okay to keep fighting for someone to love you. Perhaps that was the mistake I had been making all along, and in that very moment I decided that I didn't want to speak to Krish anymore, and right there the need to hear his voice every day somehow disappeared.

As the days passed, I enjoyed my freedom. I enjoyed not having to call anyone and being free. I realised I had a lot of healing still to do. I needed to work on myself and not be dependent on anyone for my happiness. I needed to find me once again and be safe in the knowledge that I would be okay and completely fine on my own. I remembered thinking to myself, it's the very people who you think will save you that will disappoint you the most. People may let you down and disappoint you, but never disappoint and let yourself down, because in the end, you must be your own hero in your life story. Only you can save yourself!

CHAPTER 19

As the days went on, my enjoyment of any freedom was short-lived. The pain of being frozen out by Krish caused me heart-rending despair and the grief was as though my heart had been ripped from my body. That spiritual and telepathic connection between us had also disappeared. I could feel that he had shut me off from his thoughts and shut me out of his heart. The cords between us had been cut. I had never felt pain like this before. It agonised me day and night, as I would remember the love that I had lost. They say where there is grief, there was once great love. Every evening

In the Face of All Things Unknown

I would enter my own hell. The silence of being alone within my own four walls would torture me. I would fall asleep crying into my pillow most nights, and on others I would lie awake throughout the night, getting 3 or 4 hours sleep if I was lucky. Although my heart wouldn't make a sound, it was screaming with pain. I finally understood the grief of a broken heart, and yet to the world I appeared okay. I was still breathing. If any man would appear in my dreams, Krish would be there too, haunting me, and reminding me again and again of his presence. He would not allow me to move on emotionally. The roller coaster that I was on had turned into a ghost train. I wanted to get off and hide from my reality. I wanted to pretend that I had never met him and that none of this had ever happened. However, the universe would not let me forget Krish. The memories of him were everywhere. With every song played on the radio, with the clothes and the perfumes that I had worn when with him, everything pointed back to Krish.

Three and a half months later, we still had not spoken. The inner child inside of me simply wanted to connect with him – however, my ego and hurt now stood in the way. I felt a sense of impending doom as I worried about my future and felt scared of being alone once again.

CHAPTER 20

In the wake of everything going on in my life, I felt like I had lost all sense of who I was. I was desperately trying to cling to a sense of familiarity. I needed grounding as I no longer felt secure in any aspect of my life. Other than the extremely loving bond that Zen and I shared, everything else now seemed so fickle. With Krish pulling away from me, I was forced to go further within and try to understand my own mind and my own perspective that I had formed of the world that I lived in. Relationships did not come easy to me. I was quite likeable and fun to be around, but I was just too scared to let people in. I was always vetting potential friendships, starting from a place of fear. I feared being hurt by people and therefore I was extremely choosy about who I would let in.

I wasn't proud of myself for being this way, but the only way I knew how to protect my heart was by closing off part of it. It had become a survival skill to me. So long as I could ward off potential danger and threats to my heart, I thought I would be okay. However, this heart of mine would often feel lonely. It longed for connection, and the only time it had truly managed to do this was when I was with Krish. For the first time in my life, I had felt safe being vulnerable with him. I had felt that his love for me was deep enough to see past my flaws. In fact, Krish's love had inspired me to try and be a better version of myself. He had brought out the best in me and my heart just knew that if he was capable of loving me at my worst, then he deserved to experience me when I was at my best, and I desperately wanted to be that for him. I wanted to blossom into being the best that I could possibly be.

However, now that Krish had gone, I no longer knew what to believe anymore. Just as I had almost given up my faith in love, one morning an invitation landed on my front doormat. It was an invitation to attend a reunion being held at my former school, Reddington Hill. Perhaps it was a gentle nudge from the universe, pushing me to meet up with old friends who I hadn't seen in a very long time and to rekindle our friendships. So, I decided to attend. On the day of the reunion, in true Catholic school fashion, we gathered for mass inside the beautiful school chapel. Sister O'Hara stood up to say a few words. Back in the day, she took our class for religious studies. I always did enjoy my lessons with her. Unlike all the other nuns, she was quite different in that she spoke about the love of God from a universal perspective and not just from a Christian viewpoint. She would draw examples and give context to the points that she made, using references to religious texts belonging to all faiths. Sister O' Hara allowed our minds room for questioning and seeking, which encouraged a healthy dialogue between her students and herself. Her style of teaching was all-embracing, in a 'universal love' kind of way, rather than coming from a place of indoctrination. I found it to be very refreshing and engaging.

I was intrigued what her topic would be at the school reunion address to the students. Perhaps it was a bizarre twist of fate, or synchronicity playing out at its best, but of all subjects she could have picked, Sister O'Hara chose to speak about 'Divine love' and the important role that women have in this world. She went on to say,

"The message of divine and unconditional love comes in all religions.

In the Face of All Things Unknown

God honours His creation of mankind by creating us in His own image and likeness. We are separated by Him into male and female. However, although we are distinct, we are nonetheless equally valuable as we both reflect and mirror the image and likeness of God, and yet God is only one.

Divine love is a Godly love, for it is unconditional. It is not prescriptive like the kind of societal love that we have created for ourselves. It does not judge nor does it discriminate against gender, colour, being a sinner, divorcee, widow, or single mother. After all, we are all created in the image and likeness of God. No one is superior nor are they inferior. We are all equally loved by Him.

Mary Magdalene had deep reverence for Jesus. This was most evident when she kissed the feet of her Saviour as a form of surrender. This showed her unwavering love and commitment to Him. So deep was her love that she was a loyal servant to the Divine, and so the Divine had also bestowed deep trust unto her, and that is why Jesus chose to appear to Mary Magdalene after His death, in His final revelation. They say it is because she understood His revelations more than any of the other disciples.

It is through being a loyal servant to the Divine that Mary became a Master. Today she is recognised and revered as the saint who carried on the message of Lord Jesus Christ and hence it is Mary Magdalene who carried the Christian faith on.

Mary is symbolic of being the embodiment of Christian devotion. It is through this example of Mary and Jesus that we understand that when the feminine principle and the masculine principle merge and are in unison, the message of Divine love can be delivered to all of humanity, as one cannot go on without the other."

I left the reunion rather intrigued by the whole concept of Divine love, as it had got my mind thinking. As I was walking out of the chapel towards my car, lost deep in thought, I heard somebody call out my name. I looked back, and it was my childhood friend, Dahlia. We gave each other a warm, tight hug as we were both so happy to finally be meeting after such a long time. Dahlia suggested that we catch up properly over a bite to eat at the local burger joint that we used to frequent regularly as kids. "Gosh, it's been an absolute lifetime since we last came here", said Dahlia. I replied in the affirmative, "Twenty two years to be exact." We laughed because we were both thinking just how old that made us feel and how the taste of greasy burgers and chips were no longer as appetising as they had been back then. Dahlia pulled out her phone and showed me some pictures of her five-year-old daughter. "Isha, this is Khadija, my little princess. She is my love and my absolute joy." Khadija had the same piercing bottle-green eyes as her mother and dark olive skin. She was a very pretty girl, just as her mother had been during our school days. "That's a beautiful name. What does it mean?" I asked.

"Khadija (RA: Radhi Allahu 'anha - May Allah be pleased with her) was the first wife of the Prophet Muhammed (PBUH: Peace Be Upon Him) and the first to believe in his message. She is given great reverence in Islam and is considered by many as one of history's most remarkable women." I was of course intrigued and wanted to know more about Khadija (RA) and the special role that she played in Islam and therefore asked Dahlia to explain a little more. Dahlia continued, "Khadija (RA) had many admirable qualities. She was a successful businesswoman and was known to spend her worldly riches on the poor. She supported the Prophet

(PBUH) in his ministry during the harsh opposition of his people and it was her encouragement that helped the Prophet (PBUH) believe in his mission when no one else did. It was Khadija (RA) that gave great comfort and helped the Prophet (PBUH) when there was no one else to lend him a helping hand. Although Khadija (RA) was a widow, a single mother and fifteen years elder to the Prophet (PBUH), of all his wives, she was the most beloved. Even today, Muslims across the world speak of the great love that they shared, and Khadijah (RA) is respected for her unconditional love and support of the Prophet (PBUH)." "That's incredible, I can see why you would choose such a profound name for your daughter", I said to Dahlia. She replied, "For me, Khadija (RA) is such an inspirational woman, and I can only hope that by naming my daughter after her, she grows up to value and understand her self- worth as a woman. She must not see herself as being any less than a man. After all, they are each two halves of a whole, because together they empower one another, just as the Prophet (PBUH) and his beloved wife Khadija (RA) did."

As I drove home that night, my mind kept going over and over what I had learnt earlier that day. The divinity of women as being equal and necessary to men has been talked about since the beginning of time and is referred to in most religious texts, so when did we as women start accepting a mould for ourselves which deemed us as being subordinate to men? Somewhere along the line we became pegged as being the lesser sex because it was perhaps more advantageous to men to assume the role of the superior sex, but all along we were just as important and powerful too. God had created us that way and yet we had failed to grasp and understand the very essence of the divine messages that had been sent from the very beginning of time. It made me realise that Dahlia was right – it was time for women to no longer accept and assume a lesser role. We now needed to recognise and awaken the divinity within ourselves and raise our daughters to do the same.

Upon returning home from the reunion, I was exhausted and fell asleep on the sofa, only to be woken, once again, by the loud and beautiful sound of flapping wings. I could barely keep my eyes open, but I knew that my guardian angel was trying to get my attention. Struggling to remain awake, I once again fell asleep.

The following morning, having woken up from a long and deep sleep, I was feeling rather hot and sweaty. Intuitively I knew that my guardian angel had sent me spiritual healing. My mind was well rested and receptive to the spiritual download that was intended for me. This time the message the angel shared was clear. "Let go of the hate and forgive, because that is our truest nature. Forgiveness heals. Let this illuminate the darkness within you and your very essence. Only then will you find your inner peace." As the days went by,

I kept thinking about the message that my guardian angel had delivered to me. I immersed myself in daily prayer. I prayed for strength and guidance and I prayed for clarity of thought. My mind would often start to reflect upon where my life was going and where I had gone wrong in the past. With amazing clarity, my flaws became strikingly apparent to me. Bit by bit, I now started to understand myself a little better. I realised that I had been using relationships to mask my feelings of self-hatred. These were feelings where I had lacked self-love and care for myself. In many ways, I didn't feel worthy of love. I had been repeating the same pattern for the last twenty years. I was desperately clinging on to Krish, not because of the need to feel loved, but instead I was trying to fill a void that I had created by not loving myself. It was this lack of self-love which kept bringing me to my knees every time I found myself in a relationship. I had always jumped hoops to try and win the approval of others and when that never came, I began to feel bitter inside.

Now it had finally dawned on me that I didn't need to seek approval through the eyes of others, because my eyes were good enough. They always were, but I just needed to be happy within myself for the person that I was and the person that I was growing into. I needed to be happy with my own personal growth and the trajectory that I was on. The pain that I felt from the sense of rejection in my relationships was caused by me not connecting with myself and accepting who I was. All along I had been rejecting myself. It was this lack of connection with my own self that made me feel so alone. All these years, my ego-self had been so engrossed in projecting the right impression to others that I hadn't even stopped to think about what was right for me. What was my soul's truest desire? Or my soul's truest expression? I had lost all sense of authentic self along the way. However, now, for the first time in my life, I felt at liberty to rediscover me and I felt excited at the thought of who I could become. I had always felt that I was a wildflower. A little messy and a little different, but I no longer wanted to make any excuses for my spirit that longed to dance to the beat of its own drum. I wanted to finally embrace 'Me' and let my passion burn more brightly than my fears. I wanted to be the very best of my 'authentic' self the way that God had intended all along. I wanted to fall in love with that glorious being that I always was, from deep within. And so, as I began to drop the hatred that I had carried for myself for all these years, I started to accept all of me – the light, the darkness, my imperfections and my strengths. But most of all, I had to come to terms with forgiving myself for all the years that I had wasted whilst embroiled in self-sabotage and self-hatred.

Over the next few days, I found that as I began to do this, I started to fall in love with everything connected with me – my relationships, my job, my friends, my work colleagues, my city and my country. The list was endless. I felt an overwhelming sense of appreciation and gratitude for even the smallest things around me, like the flowers in my garden that I had never noticed before, and the beautiful country roads that I travelled on each morning on the way to work. I judged less. I criticised less. I just felt open and immensely content. I realised that somewhere along the line, I had become that love I was always in search of, from someone else. I had become that love that I always wanted to receive. And as love replaced hatred in my heart, I found forgiveness for Krish too.

In the Face of All Things Unknown

CHAPTER 21

As the months rolled on, I began to feel that I had outgrown my job, the one that I had previously loved so much. I now needed a change of environment and an injection of new energy. My workplace reminded me of the time when my relationship with Krish was in that beautiful beginning phase. I remembered how, during my breaks, I would stand in the office car park and speak to Krish on the phone every day. However, this had all seemed to evaporate into thin air when he pulled away from me, and every day, pulling in and out of that same car park, reminded me of the connection that was no more. It pained my heart every moment of every day. I no longer wanted that constant reminder of Krish anymore. Strangely enough, after having completed exactly a year's service at that office, I managed to secure an incredible job, as Senior In-house Legal Counsel for a finance company in the heart of London's financial district. My salary had increased significantly, which enabled me to buy a place that Zen and I could finally call home.

One month later and on Zen's 9th birthday, I stumbled across a beautiful little bungalow that was for sale, not too far from Zen's school. When I walked into that house, I instinctively knew it was going to be our perfect home, and so I went ahead and made an offer to purchase the property. The vendor, Mrs Asare, had lived there with her husband for more than fifty years. Her husband was from Ivory Coast, and she hailed from Germany. When they had first got married, their inter-racial marriage had not been accepted by society at large. They faced a great deal of hardship and harsh judgement because of it. This home was their love nest. It had given them refuge from all the shaming and name-calling that society had put them through. I felt blessed that I had inherited a home with such history behind it. The bungalow was testament to the beauty of universal love, which is all accepting, without discrimination and without labels. I once again started to feel excited by the uncertainty that life had to offer me.

In the Face of All Things Unknown

The chalet-style bungalow was a cosy, three-bedroom abode, which sat comfortably on top of a hill, where one could capture a 360-degree view of London – you could even see as far as Canary Wharf. The bay window in the living room looked out onto the wildflowers in the garden and the glorious tilting Japanese maple tree, which draped the lawn with its deep burgundy leaves. The garden backed onto some woods called The Hogs Back and the tall oak trees in the woods seemed as if they gave shelter and privacy to the property, creating a sanctuary of peace in the garden. The bungalow was peaceful too. The energies were different here. They were comforting and soothing and every time I would return home from a day spent in the outside world, I would take a huge sigh of relief. The home felt snug. It was big enough for Zen and me to move around freely and entertain the many guests that would come to visit us, and yet it was small enough to feel safe, cosy and homely. This was perhaps the first time in my life where I had felt safe and at peace.

Each time I looked outside my window and into my garden, I would think of Krish. The leaves of the beautiful Japanese maple tree were turning fiery red in anticipation of the coming autumn. I was being reminded that yet another year was passing. I longed to be with Krish, but this time the pain was a little different. My life was filled with happiness. My new home and my new job were all fresh beginnings for me.

It was a brand-new chance at life once again. Krish was still there though, in everything. I could feel him around me and sense him. None of this would have been possible without him. I now longed for his physical presence in my life and in my home too, but most of all, I longed to share my new-found happiness with him. I wanted my two loves, Zen and Krish to also meet. I hoped that they would also grow to love each other one day, just as I loved them both. I knew Krish would have been so happy for me and so proud of how far I had come in my journey.

Months passed as I settled into our new home. There was no news from Krish – the silence was still all-too prevailing from him. And then, suddenly one day, on the way home from work, I received a text on my phone which read, "Hi, Isha. How are you?" It was from Krish. I had waited months for this day, and when it finally came, it was as though no time had passed at all between us. We exchanged a few texts and decided to meet the following day over lunch. When we met, Krish seemed a little anxious at first, but then he began to talk. He told me that I had really hurt him when I had accused him of cheating on me. It came at a time when he was facing some difficult months, both professionally and personally. I then learnt that his grandfather, whom he was particularly close to, had also died during this time. There was no anger or coldness between us. It was as though there was this gentle understanding and knowing that we had both been apart because we needed to be. We needed to go deep within ourselves first, to heal those broken parts that were causing us pain and preventing us from connecting with each other in the way that we should have been all along.

However, I soon realised that Krish and I dealt with our pain very differently. I had this overwhelming need and desire to talk and connect with him. By contrast, Krish preferred to barricade himself behind these thick, deep emotional walls which were designed to not let me in. Nor was he prepared to venture outside. That was why he had shut me off for all these months. He instead decided to withhold his feelings and detach from me. Perhaps it was easier for him to push me away. As much as I wanted to express my feelings of love towards him, I could see that he was still fearful and instead was choosing to suppress his feelings. Krish knew that I could see right through him. I could feel his frustrations and sense his fears as though they were my own. He had projected them on to me all along but failed to see that I was just the mirror reflecting to him that which he couldn't see within himself. He feared his failures – he feared that he wasn't good enough to be a part of my life. He feared that one day the veil would be lifted and perhaps I would no longer love him if I knew him too closely. There was so much hurt within him which meant that he did not allow me to get too close.

Our frequency often oscillated between the two emotions of love and fear. When in tune together with the frequency of love we were complete and in perfect harmony. But when Krish and I would give power to our fears, we would both want to control each other in a misplaced attempt to try and gain some certainty between us. However, nothing in life is certain nor can we control it. We can only live in a constant vibration of love and faith to attract all good things in our life that we truly desire and surrender our fears to the universe. Mine was undoubtedly a fear of abandonment, living alone, managing financially alone, and never having a romantic true love that I could call my own. Krish knew this, as I had shared my fears with him all along. He told me that during the time we were apart, he tried to

In the Face of All Things Unknown

shut me off, but I was constantly on his mind and that I would often come into his dreams, just as he would come into mine. But he himself realised that attempts to break away from me were futile because our connection was beyond the physical realm.

Although our bodies may not have communicated during the time that we were apart, our spirits did. Krish said he would often feel quite anxious when we weren't in touch and was worried for me. He would pray for me every single day. He prayed that I was okay and that I was doing well. He would pray that I would overcome my fears and my hardships. He also prayed that I would get a better paid job so that I could afford a home for Zen and me to live in. I then paused and realised that everything that Krish had been praying for had manifested in my life as divine blessings. Within the space of eighteen months, I had managed to draw a line under my former life and etch out a new dream for myself. With Krish's love, support and prayers, I had gone from being an underpaid, part-time sales associate to having a high-flying job in the City of London as a senior lawyer. More importantly, with the help of Krish, I had managed to buy my dream home and manifest that sense of security that I had always craved. My dream had now become a reality for me.

Nani would often tell me as a child that nothing proves that you love someone more than mentioning them in your prayers, and perhaps there was no other way that Krish could have shown me a deeper love or care than this. Krish had loved me all along, but I had failed to see it because I wasn't ready for love. I didn't even love myself, and therefore accepting love from him was near-impossible for me. I could see from his face that these months that we had been apart had been as hard for him as they had been for me. His eyes said it all. I wanted to hold him, and I wanted Krish to feel the security of my unconditional love for him. I longed for him to open his heart and reach out to me and feel safe enough to surrender his hurt and his pain. Krish had given me a new chance at life, once again, and just as his love and acceptance had nurtured me, and allowed me to be reborn, I wanted him to know that I too loved him through his strengths and his weaknesses.

I asked Krish, "So where do we go from now?" Krish remained silent. After a while he mentioned that he still wanted me to be a part of his life, but in what capacity he did not say. He told me there wasn't anyone else in his life, and my heart believed that too. I knew I could not force him to clarify things between us – I had tried before to control the uncertainty of our fate. I realised that I had to simply trust my feelings and my instincts, and that God will unite me with my true love and my divine counterpart. But, for this to happen, I just had to surrender my fear, and trust in divine timing. I needed to trust the process of it all and believe that when I was ready to receive such deep and profound love it will come back to stay. However, right now, we were both not yet aligned and healed to honour this beautiful connection between us, the way God had intended us to.

As time passed, Krish and I kept in touch, but our relationship was far from what it had been in our earlier days when we had just met. He now seemed more emotionally distant and more aloof, and I was more guarded too. A veil of fear remained between us, which we both hid behind more frequently than not. Perhaps we were both scared of reliving that agonising pain that we had felt when we were both estranged from one another during those long months. We were a lot more than friends, but still there was no label for the relationship that we now shared. We were close enough to not be too far, and yet far enough to not be too close. It wasn't just the emotional distance between us, it was the physical too. Krish had decided to take up a project in Italy which saw him moving to Santa Maria di Leuca, a coastal town in the southern region of Puglia, which forms the heel of Italy's famous southern boot. This also happened to be his grandfather's hometown. At first, he would often send me pictures of the local towns with white-washed hills that were sprawled along the Mediterranean coastline, but then eventually, all contact stopped between us.

When Krish and I were estranged from one another, the mere thought of him would haunt me, as I struggled to let go of the attachment and the longing for a future between us. It wasn't an insecurity. It was a fear of losing a love that had been so profound for me because it had put me on a journey that took me back to my maker and that touched me at the level of my soul. Once you have tasted the bliss of the divine, nothing else quite compares. However, when he was with me, I felt inspired to be the best that I could possibly be, and it propelled me into reaching new heights that I never thought were possible for me. His presence brought calm and solace to my aching soul. This was the first time that I had loved from a place of God-consciousness, and my fear was to not experience this again.

There was nothing forced about trying to love Krish. It was never a matter of convenience, or suitability, or ticking the right boxes. My love for him flowed in a way that I didn't even think was possible, because so far, I had only ever experienced love for my child in this way. It was an unconditional way of loving, that I could not stop, no matter how hard I tried. He understood my loneliness as a single mother and my insecurities and feeling of isolation. He was the one person that saw right through me and the act of bravado that I would wear each day as armour to fend off the pity-parties that would come my way. To the world I was doing "just fine" but Krish saw through my façade, frustrations and anxieties, and yet he loved me for who and what I was.

Ironically, the only way for me to let go of the expectation of Krish coming back into my life was to love more deeply. I had to love him enough to set him free, without any bitterness or reluctance on my part. I also had to love myself even more to understand that I deserved the very best, and so long as I had hope in my heart, love and care for myself, God would bring love into my life. I couldn't give up on having faith for a better tomorrow.

As the days passed, I realised that I was no longer a hostage to my fears and self-limiting beliefs. I was not scared of being alone. Instead, I was filled with the trust and joy of knowing that love cannot be chased. It can only be experienced and felt, and I felt surrounded by love, Divine love. It is often said that the best gift in life is freedom. Freedom from the constraints imposed by others, freedom of thought, freedom of spirituality, freedom of expression. But perhaps the most precious of them all is freedom from your own self-limiting beliefs and fears, because nothing can keep you stuck and imprisoned more than the four walls of your own mind.

CHAPTER 22

My 40th birthday beckoned, and I had a strong desire to travel to Jerusalem. Perhaps it was a calling to visit the most sacred sites of Christians, Jews and Muslims, the places where millions of people come together to pray within the walls of the ancient city and put their faith into something much greater than themselves, despite being divided by political and religious tension. On the second day of my journey, I decided to visit one of the holiest sites of Christendom, the Via Dolorosa, also known as the 'Way of Sorrow' or the 'Way of Suffering'. It is believed to be the path that Jesus walked

In the Face of All Things Unknown

upon, bearing the cross, on the way to His crucifixion over two thousand years ago.

Each year thousands of Christian pilgrims from around the world visit and walk along this path. It is here that they relive and celebrate the passion, death and resurrection of Christ. As I walked down the Way of Sorrow, I began to question what it must have meant for the Son of God to have carried His own cross on this very path to Calvary, and to the site of His own crucifixion. Jesus, the one whom we call upon for help, whom we consider to be our strength, was Himself being subjected to the humiliation of falling down in weakness as He struggled to bear the heavy weight of the cross. Often in life, we too are called upon to carry the weight of our own cross. We may find that we stumble and fall many times, especially when we fall under the weight of our own suffering, which is the ultimate test of our faith. We may call upon others to help us along the way. Loved ones may support us, pray for us, and do whatever they can to make our lives better and distract us from our pain, but they cannot prevent our suffering. Ultimately, we must face our fears alone – our humiliation, our heartbreak, and our pain alone. When you are weak and worn, we are all faced with the same question: what will you do with your pain and suffering?

It is not enough to just survive the suffering, but instead one must have hope to come out of it at the other end, better and more 'whole'. It is a healing process, to have grown in our faithfulness and love for God, for ourselves and for our neighbours. In this journey we call life, we must find our way back to ourselves and to our Source – our divine maker. He was always present, waiting for us to call upon Him and surrender our pain to Him, and if there is faith, then on the other side of all this human suffering is a fresh beginning and a new chance at life for all of us.

In the Face of All Things Unknown

CHAPTER 23

As we entered the new year of 2020, news of the novel coronavirus (Covid-19), which had originated in Wuhan, China, became more prevalent. The Chinese government had reported that their nation had gone into lockdown on 23rd January. At that point, it still seemed far away and in too far a distant country to have been at the forefront of our lives. However, within weeks it brought Italy to a state of emergency and by March, Italy was in lockdown. Northern Italy had been hardest hit, more than the south. The number of recorded deaths was rising at an alarming rate and within days the numbers had risen to thousands.

Watching the news every day got me into a state of anxiety and panic. Krish hadn't been in touch for months and I needed to know that he was okay. I kept calling his number, but each attempt was met by an answerphone message. I then wrote him an email and prayed for a response. Days passed and there was no answer. I had no way of knowing if he was alive and well, but if the media reports were being cited accurately, every household was under a strict curfew and each street was being monitored by the police. By 23rd March, the UK followed suit and also went into lockdown. It felt like a new order was being created throughout the world. A rebalancing of some sort. As humans were forced to stay at home and indoors, nature finally had the chance to thrive. There were reports around the world of pollution levels decreasing, especially in the most populous cities. Fish could now clearly be seen in the once cloudy waters of the canals of Venice. Without the sound of the car engines the only sound to be heard outside the front door was the melodious chirping of birds. Unlike us, the birds seemed happy and unaffected. The world was much the same for them, perhaps even better now.

Fear had taken a grip over each household. There was nowhere one could escape to. We were being imprisoned within our homes, held hostage by a silent enemy that nobody could see. The virus was relentless. In a matter of weeks, it had ripped through the heart of the country, mercilessly claiming the lives of thousands. Covid-19 did not discriminate between the young or the old, although the former seemed to have a better chance of coming through the other end unscathed. As everyone stared mortality in the eye, panic buying of medicine and food had ensued in supermarkets and chemists. We began preparing for devastation of apocalyptic proportions. Meanwhile, in Italy, stories were emerging of food shortages. People were unable to work and all too soon, their savings had run dry. Fights were breaking out in the streets, as people became so hungry and desperate to feed the stomachs of their families. Where was Krish? Why had he not replied to me. I worried about Krish constantly. Was he okay? Was he well? Had he fallen ill with the virus? The questions were many, but there was no one to answer them.

Day in, day out, the news channels only told of the grim reality of the pandemic that the world was facing. Sick and tired of only hearing the constant stream of negativity, I vowed not to watch the news ever again. However, what kept me tuned in one evening was the special coverage being shown on the state of northern Italy, by a renowned British journalist and her crew. The presenter wanted to highlight the great difficulties and dangers that were posed in putting this piece of coverage together. As a team they wanted to reach the far and forgotten corners of Italy and expose those pockets where people were really suffering and being taken advantage of by the opportunist mafia. People were now so hungry that they were willing to accept bribes from the mafia and turn to drug dealing, just to put food on the table for their families. As the presenter introduced each member that made up her crew, she then introduced the man behind the camera. It was none other than Krish. He was alive and well, but his eyes seemed incredibly sad. Relieved to now know that Krish was okay, I contacted the news channel and told them that Krish was a missing friend and that I'd spotted him on their news channel and needed to make contact with him urgently.

In the Face of All Things Unknown

Three days later, I received an email from a lady called Caitlin. She told me that Krish was safe and doing well and that due to the nature of their work and constant movement, Krish had lost his mobile phone and had been given a replacement one instead. She also explained that they had limited internet access which is probably why I had not heard from him via email either. She gave me Krish's new number and I called him immediately. There was a long pause when he answered the phone, followed by a deep sigh. I was so pleased to hear that it was a sigh of relief and that Krish was extremely happy to hear from me.

"I've seen some terrible things, Isha. Even though there is a distance between us of thousands of miles, you have been there with me in everything, in every second and in every moment. It was the hope to meet you again that got me through my darkest days. Every day I have seen people lying on their death beds. Some were far too ill to talk, and others were just scraping by, knowing that death could be imminent. I have heard countless tales of lives lived with regret, by many just before they have died. I have also spoken with those who have lost their loved ones during this pandemic and not had the chance to say goodbye. They have all said many things, but you know what they all had in common? They wished that they had expressed their love more freely to their loved ones and spent more time with them. They wished that they had made more time for travel and adventure and they wished that they had listened to their heart more and their ego less. I realised that 'love' is God's benevolence, and when it comes knocking at your door, you don't turn it away, as I have done. When I turned my back on you, it was as though I had turned my back on God. I have tried so hard to forget you, and the fear of loving you and accepting your love kept me running. I have been running for a long time from you, but mostly from myself. What you made my heart feel, scared me because I had never known it to be capable of such love. I feared being hurt again. I don't want to run anymore. I don't want to keep running away from where it is that I want to get to. But most of all, I don't want our story to end here. I want to walk alongside you in life – I want to care for you, and I want to love you. So, before we get lost again, can we start over and forget our past? Let us look to the future as if it has always been just you and me. Isha, will you allow me to love you once again? This time I want us to be a family, you, Zen, and me, together."

I was quiet on the end of the phone as I took in the enormity of everything Krish had just said. There was nothing more that I wanted for myself and Zen than to share our lives with him, and nothing would have made me happier. However, we both knew that it would take some time before the world would return to a new sense of normality.

In the Face of All Things Unknown

Ten months passed, and then, in a small and beautiful ceremony held in Lake Como, Krish and I were married before our loved ones. Not that long after our nuptials we also celebrated the arrival of a little sister for Zen. We named her Meher, which means 'benevolence' because for us she was God's benevolence. Krish was the most wonderful father to our children. He was loving, caring, gentle and supportive, just as he was with me. He was very much just as my heart had recognised and understood him to be all along. After many months, things began to settle at home too. There was a great awakening of the sleeping consciousness of the world, and a new order was setting in. The pandemic had reminded us of our collective vulnerability and even our finitude. There was now a new appreciation for all that we took for granted in life – our relationships, our health and mental wellbeing, but most of all, the appreciation for living each day as it came, because tomorrow was never promised. I was happy that my children would be growing up in a world far different to the one that I had known as a child. Sometimes everything we know, and life as we know it, needs to break away for something new to emerge, something even better!

In the Face of All Things Unknown

ABOUT THE AUTHOR

Shilpe is a lawyer by profession and a mother of one. She was born in October 1979, in the suburbs of North-West London and still resides there to this day.

From a young age, she had a vivid imagination and loved writing stories. However, it wasn't until her late thirties, that Shilpe began to take this creative expression of hers more seriously.

Writing and journaling became a place of solace for Shilpe as she navigated through uncharted waters during a turbulent and difficult period in her life. In many ways, it helped her to reconnect with herself and her surroundings.

It was these very notes written during this time, which inspired Shilpe to write this novel and take you on Ishas' journey, as she experiences life **In The Face of All Things Unknown!**

When Shilpe isn't writing, she can be found exploring nature trails and going on hikes. She is a seeker at heart and loves adventure, travel, and meeting people from all walks of life.

For more information about Shilpe, log on to www.shilpenanda.com

Printed in Dunstable, United Kingdom